香 爱

The Fragrant Love

[汉英对照]

曾 抗 著

Kang Zeng

长江出版传媒

长江文艺出版社

目　录

第三辑　风恶轻薄 / 227

第一辑　闭月羞花

眼　睛

你有春天的眼睛
水晶般清澈透明
躲闪的眼神里
藏不住遥远的憧憬
细雨洒落心底
不露一丝痕迹
感觉如此神秘
叫人怎么不着迷

你有夏天的眼睛
太阳般灿烂
让人无法阻拦
火辣辣把欲望点燃
在野性的碰撞中
战栗目眩
残阳如血
慢慢闭上眼

你有秋天的眼睛
双瞳剪水
剪不断秋水幽幽
流淌成两个荡漾的湖面
泛起一层水雾
罩不住相思的朦胧

Eyes

Your eyes are like spring,
Crystal clear and transparent.
Evasive eyes
Can not hide the distant longing.
The fine rain falls to the bottom of my heart
Without an imprint.
I am so infatuated
With your mysterious eyes.

Your eyes are like summer,
Shining as bright as the sun,
Which can not be hidden.
My desire is ignited by your eyes,
In the wild collision of two bodies,
I tremble and feel dizzy.
The setting sun makes the sky as red as blood
And we close our eyes slowly.

Your eyes are like autumn,
Clear and bright.
The autumn water continues flowing,
Becoming two rippling lakes.
The mist over the lakes
Can not cover the hazy lovesickness.

我愿溺在其中
沉睡不醒

你有冬天的眼睛
雪花飞舞
飘落进去
流出冷却的泪珠
不经意间凝结成冰
冻结了时空
执着的背后
我懂

2017.2.13

I would like to drown in it
And sleep there forever.

Your eyes are like winter.
When the fluttering snowflakes
Fall into your eyes,
They will become into cold tears.
Unconsciously they turn into ice,
Freezing the time and space.
Behind your persistence,
There is my understanding.

February 13, 2017

头　发

她从闺房里出来
乌黑的头发瀑布般倾泻
衬托着雪白的香腮
在凝脂的肌肤上自然散开

她从花丛里走来
浓密的云发把春色覆盖
小指轻轻钩起唇边的几缕发丝
不经意露出娇羞的神态

她从海边走来
海风吹乱了修长的云发
刘海下面藏不住美丽的眼睛
装满大海般的柔情和期待

她从浴室里出来
一头湿漉漉亮丽的秀发
散发着香气
静静等待他趁着夜色赶来

2017.7.17

Hair

She walks out of her bedroom
With black hair pouring down like a waterfall
Which flows on the creamy skin,
Setting off her white fragrant cheek.

She comes out of the flowers
And the thick cloud of hair covers the beauty of spring.
She flips a few strands of hair near her lips,
Carelessly exposing her shyness.

She arises out of the sea
And her long hair is disheveled by the sea wind.
Her beautiful eyes under her bang
Are filled with the ocean of tenderness and expectation.

She walks out of the bathroom
With wet and bright hair
Which is giving off the aroma.
She is waiting quietly for his arrival tonight.

July 17, 2017

手

手是你的第二张脸
花儿似的绽放在春天
丰满红润，灵巧精致
柔弱无骨，圆圆软软
纤纤白皙，滑腻修长
轻轻地，握着温暖
不经意，交合着缠绵
描龙绣凤，美轮美奂
拨弄琴弦，惊艳了寂寞的夜晚
典雅玲珑的戒指，把爱情镶嵌
杏仁般的指甲，比象牙还洁净好看
如天上的星星，亮闪闪
多想捧起你美丽的双手
告诉你，别离开我的视线

2018.1.20

Hands

Your hands are your second face,

Blooming quietly in spring.

They are plump, ruddy, graceful and exquisite.

They are delicate, round and soft.

They are white, velvety and slender.

You gently grasp the warmth

And cross your fingers to show your feelings inadvertently.

Do the fine needlework beautifully.

Pluck the strings to make the lonely night amazing.

The elegant exquisite ring is inlaid with love.

The almonds-like fingernails are purer than ivory,

Bright as the stars in the sky.

I want to hold both of your beautiful hands,

And tell you not to get out of sight.

January 20, 2018

足

凹凸有形，雕刻出艺术的精品
柔弱无骨，踩出大地春天的乐曲
像两只柔顺乖巧的小白兔，嫩嫩盈盈
脚背上几道淡青，迷惑了昨夜依稀的梦境
浑圆的足踝，把春天涂抹成粉红
轻弯的脚弓，弹出了一弯柔情
晶莹剔透、匀称秀丽的脚趾
是十个精致的小姊妹，暧昧含情
似十个静静透明的蚕宝宝，乖乖卖萌
如十朵竞相绽放的小花，生香轻轻
你是上帝赐予的礼物，给我无尽的遐想
轻轻捧在手中，又怕呼吸吹破了你美妙的憧憬
你吸天地之灵气，妩媚走来
走进我的心海，轻盈入梦

2017.2.14

Feet

You are a work of art with a beautiful shape.

You are delicate but play the music of spring ground.

You're like two little clever limber white rabbits, tender and plump.

Several light blue blood vessel on the foot instep, confusing last
    night's faint dream.

Perfectly round ankles are painting spring pink.

The foot arches are like two bays of tender feelings.

Crystal-clear and shapely toes

Are ten delicate little sisters, full of ambiguous feelings.

They're ten quiet transparent baby silkworms, acting cute obediently.

They're like ten blooming flowers, breathing fragrance gently.

You are God's gift and give endless reverie to me.

Holding you gently in my hands, I'm afraid my breath will shatter
    your wonderful vision.

With the sensitivity of heaven and earth, you're walking towards me
    charmingly,

Walking into my heart and into my dream lightly.

February 14, 2017

背

远远地，我不敢向前
你的妙曼玉背，婀娜翩跹
曲线出风情万千
怕我的出现，惊扰了你
耐人寻味的神秘感

远远地，我不敢向前
你的削肩玉背，一抹迷人的香艳
一对美丽的蝴蝶骨，振翅欲飞
怕我的出现，打扰了他俩双双的爱恋
扑棱着飞进春天

远远地，我不敢向前
你的柳腰玉背，水蛇般柔软
摆动出韵致，扭转出性感
怕我的出现，打扰了小蛮腰
冬日里缱绻的思念

远远地，我不敢向前
你的凝脂玉背，吹弹可破
让人感叹，令人生怜
怕我的出现，有忍不住的触摸感
无法体味出你美丽的质感

Back

Standing from afar, I dare not go forward.
Your exquisite and long jade-like back is graceful and lively,
Curving the myriad amorous feelings.
I'm afraid my presence will disturb your
Intriguing mystery.

Standing from afar, I dare not go forward.
The sloping shoulders of your jade-like back is charming.
A pair of beautiful butterfly ribs are desiring to fly.
I'm afraid my appearance will disturb their love
And make them flap their wings and fly away.

Standing from afar, I dare not go forward.
Your jade-like back and narrow waist are as soft as a water snake,
Swaying elegantly and twisting sexily.
I'm afraid my appearance will disturb the deep longing in winter
Of your narrow pretty waist.

Standing from afar, I dare not go forward.
Your jade-like back is creamy, smooth and fair.
I sigh with emotion and feel you're so lovingly.
I'm afraid I can't help but touch
Instead I can't appreciate your beautiful texture.

远远地，我不敢向前
你的梦幻玉背，罩住了我的呼吸
头晕目眩，忘记了时间
咬一口苹果，我不敢下咽
怕不经意间你会消失不见

2017.11.2

Standing from afar, I dare not go forward.

Your dreamy jade-like back covers my breath,

Making me dizzy and forget about the time.

I take a bite of an apple but dare not swallow.

I'm afraid you will inadvertently disappear.

November 2, 2017

性　感

性感是春天的花朵，娇艳
让人垂涎欲滴，流连忘返
性感是夏日的暴雨，肆无忌惮
雨后留下一道彩虹，七彩绚烂
性感是秋天的苹果，丰满
咬一口，脆脆甜甜
性感是冬天里的火炉，温暖
蜷缩在旁边，无尽缠绵
性感是气质的内涵，只可意会不可言传
性感是邂逅的回眸一笑，是形体美不经意的展现
性感与美丽相提并论，同妩媚肩并肩
性感是妖精的转世，风骚的代言
性感是缘分的遇见，是爱情生命力的源泉

2018.7.29

Sex Appeal

Sex appeal is the flower of spring, fresh and beautiful,

Which makes people drool and linger.

Sex appeal is the rainstorm in summer, unbridled,

Leaving a rainbow after the rain, colorful and gorgeous.

Sex appeal is the apple of autumn, plump,

Each bite tastes crisp and sweet.

Sex appeal arise the stove in winter, warm,

Beside which the lovers hold each other closely, making love endlessly.

Sex appeal stands for temperament,

Which can be sensed but not expressed in words.

Sex appeal arises when you meet her by chance

And she looks back at you with a smile,

Casually showing off her physical beauty.

Sex appeal brackets with beauty together

And is comparable with charm.

Sex appeal is the reincarnation of an alluring woman

And it is the spokesperson of flirtatious behavior.

Sex appeal is the encountering destiny

And it is the source of love's vitality.

July 29, 2018

高跟鞋

你是移动的风景
世界因你而不同
挺胸收腹翘臀
展示优雅，自信从容

你是移动的风景
支撑起女人梦，憧憬
虚幻的高度中
期待与白马王子热情相拥

你是移动的风景
装满女人的柔情
醉人的女人香
嗅着青春一路前行，轻盈

你是移动的风景
诱惑的黑夜里
被女人踢掉，轻松
恣意生命的原始冲动

你是移动的风景
走过春暖花开
穿过雨巷朦胧
红尘中孤傲独行

High-heeled Shoes

You are a moving landscape
And the world is different because of you.
A woman's chest out, stomach in, buttocks out
Help her show her grace, confidence and poise.

You are a moving landscape,
Supporting a woman's longing dream.
In an imaginary height,
She is looking forward to warmly embracing her Prince Charming.

You are a moving landscape
Which is full of a woman's tenderness.
The intoxicating scent of a woman
Is guiding the youth to go forward lightheartedly all the way.

You are a moving landscape,
In the night of temptation,
A woman kicks you off to relax
The primitive impulse of a wayward life.

You are a moving landscape
Which walks through the blossoms of spring
And goes through the hazy rain of autumn.
You walk alone and proudly in the world.

你是移动的风景
是上帝派来的爱的精灵
哒哒声牵引着我的灵魂
走入你的梦境，不醒

2017.1.26

You are a moving landscape

Which is the spirit of love that sent by God.

The rattling sound you make entices my soul

To walk into your dream and never wake up.

January 26, 2017

口　红

涂一抹口红
释放浪漫的口香
幻想遥远的爱情

涂一抹口红
开启五彩缤纷的双唇
诱惑欲望的光临

涂一抹口红
滋润岁月
闪亮在纸醉金迷的红尘

涂一抹口红
穿上女人第二件衣裳
纪念暗下去的青春时光

涂一抹口红
掩饰寂寞的灵魂
覆盖淡淡的忧伤

涂一抹口红
咽下你离别的背影
吞噬思念的苍穹

Lipstick

Apply lipstick
To release the romantic fragrance of the mouth
And fantasize about the faraway love.

Apply lipstick
To open her colorful lips
And seduce the desire to come.

Apply lipstick
To nourish the life
And shine in the world of luxury.

Apply lipstick
To put on her second dress
And commemorate the hidden days of youth.

Apply lipstick
To conceal the loneliness of the soul.
And cover the faint sadness.

Apply lipstick
To swallow up the parting figure
And the longing for the sky.

涂一抹口红
给长不好的伤口撒点盐
让生命在痛苦中永恒

2017.1.31

Apply lipstick

To put some salt on the incurable wound

And make life last in pain.

January 31, 2017

秋天姑娘

风儿冷却了热浪
大地披上了彩色衣裳
穿过枯萎的篱笆墙
去寻找你——秋天的姑娘
静静的河边没有你
茂密的芦苇随风荡漾
公园的长凳上没有你
上边一片落叶金黄
一望无际的田野上没有你
一排排玉米手持手榴弹在站岗
山脚下的果园里没有你
红彤彤的苹果丰满飘香
熙攘的街道上没有你
成群的都市姑娘笑声朗朗
你到底在哪里啊
我的秋天好姑娘
我只好把你画在油画布上
画出你丰满成熟的模样
我把你写在书法里
挥毫泼墨你的沧桑
我把你唱在歌声里
唱出你的明快和爽朗
我把你跳在舞蹈里
舞出你的风韵和倜傥

Autumn Girl

The wind has cooled the heat wave
And the earth is clothed in color.
I go across the withered hedgerow
To look for you—the autumn girl.
You are not by the quiet river
Because the thick reeds are waving in the wind.
You're not on the park bench,
On which there is a golden fallen leaf.
You are not in the endless field
As the rows of corn are standing guard with grenades.
You are not in the orchard at the foot of the hill
As the bright red apples are giving off ample fragrance.
You're not on the bustling street
Where the crowds of city girls are laughing.
My kind autumn girl,
Where on earth are you?
I have to draw you on the canvas,
Drawing your plump and mature appearance.
I write you in my Chinese calligraphy,
Writing down the transformations in your life.
I put you in my song,
Singing about your brightness and cheerfulness.
I put you in my dance,
Performing your charm and elegance.

我把你写在诗歌里

抒发你淡淡的忧伤

秋日私语里泪水凝结成霜

冷雨敲窗中把心中的满月隐藏

你说你一直住在我的心坎上

可我漫步在仲秋里

到处是你涂抹的美丽女人色

和你散发的诱人女人香

我的秋天好姑娘啊，你可知道

这让我妒忌、寂寞和彷徨

2018.9.12

I write you in my poem,

Expressing your subtle sadness.

My tears have turned into frost in the whisper of autumn.

The full moon in my heart has hidden in the cold rain which is

hitting at the window.

You have told me that you've always loved me,

But when I walk during the mid-autumn days,

All around are the beautiful colors you paint.

And the tantalizing aroma you give off.

My lovely autumn girl, you should know

This makes me jealous, lonely and confused.

September 12, 2018

女人花

心中，种一朵女人花
懵懂春天，悄悄发芽
含苞待放，羞羞答答
一阵春风，轻拂脸颊
默默绽放，香飘天涯
美丽娇柔的女人花啊
玉、雪和水是你的骨肉
清风已来，你已盛开
你的美让人窒息和怜爱
明媚艳丽的女人花啊
你是人间的尤物
枝蔓摇曳，暗香盈袖
全身溢满性感的艳波
心底生出的女人花啊
你美得像一首抒情诗
沉鱼落雁，闭月羞花
花容月貌里藏着风姿绰约
让人心疼的女人花啊
你四季轮回，花开花落
不经意间凋零飘落
怎能不让人更加留恋
万种风情的女人花啊
你在红尘中摇曳
是人间最亮丽的风景画

Woman Flower

Plant a seed of woman flower in the heart

And she sprouts quietly in ignorant spring.

She is budding and shy.

A spring breeze kisses her face gently.

She blooms silently and her fragrance floats afar.

The beautiful and delicate woman flower

Is made of jade, snow and water.

The breeze has come and you have bloomed.

Your beauty makes me breathless and feel tender.

The beautiful and voluptuous woman flower

Is the apple of my eye.

You sway your branches and emit the fragrance.

Your whole body is full of sexy temptation of love.

The woman flower which grows from my heart

Is as beautiful as a lyric.

Your beauty makes the fish sink, wild geese fall, the moon dark and
    the flowers blush for shame.

Your charming appearance and personality hides in the beauty of the
    flower and moon.

The woman flower which makes me love dearly

Blooms and fades in the four seasons.

You wither and fall inadvertently,

Which makes me more reluctant to leave you.

The woman flower has 10 thousand kinds of amorous feelings.

You sway in the world of mortals.

You are the most beautiful landscape painting in the world.

我愿是绿叶，把你衬托
我心仪的女人花啊
让我做一回护花使者吧
用毕生守护你的花期

2018.7.6

I wish I were a leaf to make you more beautiful.

My ideal woman flower,

Please allow me to be your flower guardian,

Guarding your blossoms all my life.

July 6, 2018

温柔女人

轻轻地，你来了
婀娜的身姿，飘逸的长裙
修长圆润的手臂
勾住了时光的流淌
温暖的胸怀
消融了大地的冰霜
双眸里的温柔
融化了高山上的石头
呵气如兰
吹开了春天的笑脸
温柔似水的女人啊
我愿变成一只蜜蜂
采撷你花一样的清香
我愿变成十五的月光
笼罩在你曼妙的身上
亲吻你每一寸的芬芳
我愿变成一只小船
任你随意摇晃，心甘情愿
淹没在你温柔的海洋

2017.3.19

Tender Woman

Wearing a long dress,
You gently walk
With a graceful posture.
Your slender arms
Can stop the time from elapsing.
Your warm embrace
Can thaw the earth's frost.
The tenderness in your eyes
Can melt the rocks on the high mountain.
The orchid fragrance of your body
Can bloom the smile of spring.
Ah, you are as tender as water.
I would like to be a bee,
Collecting the fragrance of your flower-like body.
I would like to become the moonlight,
Enveloping your agile and graceful body,
Kissing every inch of your body.
I would like to be a boat,
To be shaken according to your will,
To be drown willingly
In your tender ocean.

March 19, 2017

秋女人

曾经，到处找你
在春天的草地上
在夏日的荷池边
在冬天纷飞的雪花里
以为再也见不到你
今天却与你不期而遇
原来你变成了湛蓝的天空
温柔地把云朵轻轻相拥
你变成了火红的枫叶
把万里群山装点
你变成了清澈的湖水
微风中波光潋滟
你变成了红红的高粱
羞涩低头聆听风儿的歌唱
你变成了金黄的稻田
晨风中散发出阵阵清香
你变成了一串串紫色的葡萄
任凭露珠在你身上翻滚嬉闹
你变成了一缕缕炊烟
沿着阡陌小路袅袅升起
你变成了一片片飘落的叶子
化作泥土孕育春天的希望
秋天，是爱的色彩
成熟，是爱的境界

Autumn Woman

I have been looking for you everywhere,

In the grass of spring,

Beside the lotus pool of summer

And in the falling snowflakes of winter.

I thought I would not meet you again

But I met you today by chance.

You have turned into the blue sky,

Embracing the clouds tenderly.

You have become the red maple leaves,

Dressing up the mountains

You have become a clear lake,

Glittering in the breeze.

You have become red sorghum,

Shyly looking down and listening to the wind singing.

You have turned into the golden rice field,

Emitting the faint scent in the morning breeze.

You have become a bunch of purple grapes,

Allowing the dew to roll on your body.

You have become a column of smoke,

Rising fairly along the winding paths.

You have become a falling leaf,

Turning into soil to produce the hope of spring.

Fall is the color of love

And being ripe is the state of love.

心仪的秋女人啊
你多彩深沉的爱
让我如何不痴狂
我要奔向你的博大苍茫
拥抱你的丰满、明智和坚强
亲吻你的美丽、温柔和善良
在你温暖的怀抱里
感受爱情的甜蜜和芬芳
你是上帝赐给我的最大奖赏
我的灵魂从此不再彷徨
我的思念随着秋水疯长
我俩的爱情地久天长

2017.10.2

Dear, my favorite autumn woman,

Your colorful and deep love

Makes me crazy.

I'll head for your vastness,

Embracing your fullness, wisdom and strength,

Kissing your beauty, tenderness and kindness.

In your warm arms,

I'll feel the sweetness and fragrance of love.

You are the greatest reward that God has given me.

From now on, my soul will not wander any longer,

My longing is growing madly like the autumn water

And our love will be everlasting.

October 2, 2017

水女人

女人是一滴露珠
灵性晶莹
水是她的骨肉
落在地上悄然无声
让人心疼

女人是一口井水
幽深清凉
享受寂寞，拥抱孤单
守候属于自己的一方蓝天
奉献给世人清冽甘甜

女人是一片春雨
淅淅沥沥
飘逸朦胧，清新浪漫
滋润干涸的大地
给万物带来生机无限

女人是一条小溪
潺潺流淌
弯弯曲曲，以柔克刚
平淡岁月里过滤点点忧伤
用柔弱的躯体把生命之歌唱响

Water Woman

A woman is a drop of dew
Which is spiritual and crystal-clear.
Water is her flesh and blood
Which falls to the ground quietly,
Making people love dearly.

A woman is the water of a well
Which is deep, cool and refreshing.
She enjoys and hugs loneliness,
Holding fast to her own small blue sky
And dedicating the cool and sweet water to the world.

A woman is a spring rain
Which falls unhurriedly,
Graceful, hazy, fresh and romantic,
Moistening the dry earth
And bringing colorful life to all things.

A woman is a stream
Which is gurgling,
Meandering and overcoming hardness through softness.
She filters the sadness through the day-to-day life,
Using her weak body to sing the song of life.

女人是一眼温泉
从大地深处汩汩涌出
热气腾腾，水雾弥漫
洗涤风尘，消除疲倦
给人温暖，让人依恋

女人是一汪湖水
清澈宽广
涟漪微微荡漾
波平似镜下面
躲藏着幽幽的遐想

女人是太平洋
容纳百川，惊涛骇浪
稀释了寂寞，包容着过往
承载爱的小船
朝阳中勇敢扬帆远航

2017.7.25

Handbag

A beautiful handbag

Is filled with the spring scenery of a woman's life.

It includes a mobile phone, cash, ID cards, credentials, keys, makeup, an umbrella,

A pair of sunglasses, a piece of chewing gum and everything she needs.

It collects the fashionable objects to color the dull time.

It controls the emotions and embraces the romance in the dream.

It is like a woman's intimate lover who meets her emotional attachment.

It is like a close girlfriend who knows her well and never dislikes her.

It is like a private stylist who makes the finishing touches to her appearance.

It is like a woman's amulet which guards her peace of mind.

It is like a woman's world by which a man is always puzzled.

It is like a woman's baby whom others cannot touch.

It is part of a woman's body and it is always with her.

You see, a handbag knows a woman, but who can understand it?

July 18, 2017

花　瓶

即使，是一个花瓶
也要身姿曼妙，玉树临风
完美无瑕的世界里
让人欣赏，让人珍惜
爱你的人会懂

即使，是一个花瓶
也要把美丽端坐成永恒
静默成诗，泪落无声
只为守候
一瓶春天的梦

即使是一个花瓶
也要高贵典雅，一副尊容
纵然从高处突然落下
也要碎成一地剔透晶莹
留给人间无尽的心疼

2017.3.13

Vase

Even if you are a vase,
You should be beautiful,
Lithe and graceful.
In the perfect world,
People who love you
understand, appreciate and cherish you.

Even if you are a vase,
You should stay beautiful forever.
You are silent as a poem
And your tears fall silently.
You are waiting,
For your secret dream of spring.

Even if you are a vase,
You should be noble
And elegant with honor.
Even though you fall from a height suddenly,
You will break into pieces of crystal,
Leaving the endless pain to the world.

March 13, 2017

香　水

窗外，夜色阑珊
洗完澡，睡衣丝滑柔软
两支红蜡烛，点燃
暧昧的柔光，忽明忽暗
花瓶里几枝红玫瑰
在梳妆台上，静静开放
床头旁的留声机里
轻缓的音乐在流淌
拿出馨香馥郁的香水
喷在手腕、耳后根和后颈部
只要你亲吻到的地方
让卧室洒满爱的清香
是上帝对我的奖赏
知道只有你
才能意会我爱的密码
好好把我欣赏
我要把梦里你帅气的模样
涂上深夜女人香
哪怕你的声音
我也要涂满香水的芬芳
一阵清香袭来
我以为你来到我身旁
身边却只有宽大的床
抱起枕头，丝丝的忧伤

Perfume

Out of the window, the night is dim.

Having taken a shower, I put on silky and soft pajamas.

Two red candles are lit

And they are flickering.

Several red roses in the vase

Are in full bloom quietly on the dresser.

Soft music comes slowly

From the phonograph bedside the bed.

I take out the beautiful perfume

And spray it on my wrist, ear lobe and back of my neck

Where you will kiss and make the bedroom

Full of the fragrance of love.

This is God's reward for me.

I know only you can sense

The password of my love

And appreciate me well.

I will paint your elegant appearance

In my dream with woman's fragrance at night.

I will even paint perfume fragrance

On your voice.

A burst of fragrance hits me

And I thought it was you who came to me.

But there is only a large bed.

Holding the pillow, I feel a little sad.

想起你的味道
你说闻香识女人
为何让我等待在闺房

2017.3.8

Your smell comes to my mind.

You told me you could know a woman by smelling her perfume.

Why do you let me wait in my bedroom?

March 8, 2017

第二辑　思之如狂

衣 裳

裁一米阳光
照亮心房
心房里挂满思念的衣裳
随便拿一件穿在身上
温馨暖洋洋
忘了痛苦与忧伤

2017.7.16

Clothes

Take one meter of sunshine
To light my heart.
My heart is full of clothes
Which are made by my longing.
You can put on these clothes anytime
Which will make you feel warm and sweet
And forget your pain and sorrow.

July 16, 2017

你不会知道我多么爱你

你不会知道，我多么爱你
我藏在春天的花朵里
在通往你家的小路上默默盛开，等你
等你偶尔停下脚步，俯身闻我
我也好，偷偷亲吻你

你不会知道，我多么爱你
我藏在夏日的微风里
在骄阳下的街道上，等你
等你匆匆的脚步声响起
我便上前，轻轻吹掉你脸上的汗滴

你不会知道我多么爱你
我藏在秋天的菊花酒里
用思念陈酿着甜蜜，等你
等你劳作后把我轻轻端起
缓解你疲惫的身躯

你不会知道我多么爱你
我藏在冬日纷飞的雪花里
静静飘落在你的梦里，陪你
陪你深夜里的孤寂
早晨太阳一出我便悄悄离去

2017.6.12

You Do Not Know How Much I Love You

You do not know how much I love you
Because I'm hiding in the spring flowers.
I'm blooming quietly on the path leading to your house, waiting for you,
Waiting for you to stop and smell me once in a while
So that I can kiss you secretly.

You do not know how much I love you
Because I'm hiding in the summer breeze.
I'm on the sunny street, waiting for you,
Waiting for the sound of your hasty footsteps approaching.
Then I'll run to you and gently blow the sweat off your face.

You do not know how much I love you
Because I am hiding in autumn's chrysanthemum wine.
I'm making nectar with my love, waiting for you,
Waiting for you to sip me after work
So that I can relieve your exhausted body.

You do not know how much I love you
Because I'm hiding in the falling snowflakes of winter.
I'm landing silently in your dream, accompanying you,
Accompanying you in your lonely night.
And I'll leave you quietly when the sun comes out in the morning.

June 12, 2017

相　遇

白云遇到了清风
花朵遇到了太阳
我遇到了梦里的你
这是我的福气
把你的名字
轻轻写在我的花季
错过了太多的风景
幸好这次与你相逢
也许是故意
也许是擦肩的偶遇
知道你终究会离去
但我还是记住了你的美丽
在我最好的时光里

2017.5.31

The Encounter

As the white cloud encounters the breeze

And the flower encounters the sun,

I encounter you in my dream.

It is a blessing

In my dream

And I write your name gently

In my flowering season.

I missed a lot of sceneries

But fortunately I meat you this time.

Maybe it is intentional.

Maybe it is by chance.

I know you will leave me in the end

But I will still remember your beauty

In my best time.

May 31, 2017

情窦初开

走在四季路上
与春天撞了个满怀
她捧在手里的六粒花种子
被我不小心撞撒
羞愧的我马上弯腰想捡起
却怎么也捡不起来
立春的种子落在了奶奶家的小院
长成一棵枝条细长的迎春花儿
静静在窗外绽放蛋黄
雨水的种子落在了杏花村
长成村头一行行杏花树
杏花像搽了胭脂竞相开放
惊蛰的种子落在了桃花谷
长成桃林百里长
桃花春深似海千里香
春分的种子落在了家乡的山冈旁
长成满山遍野的梨树绕村庄
梨花浪花般随风荡漾
清明的种子落在小河边
长成一溜弯弯的柳树站河边
柳花摇摆，满河飘香
谷雨的种子落在牡丹园里
长成牡丹花一片国色天香
蝴蝶蜜蜂嬉戏忙

First Awakening Love

Walking on the footpath of seasons,
I ran into spring head on.
She was holding six flower seeds in her hands.
I wasn't careful and bumped into her, causing her to drop them.
Being ashamed, I immediately bent down to pick them up
However, I could not.
The seed of the Beginning of Spring fell into grandma's courtyard
And grew into a winter jasmine with slender branches
Which was light yellow and bloomed outside the window.
The seed of Rain Water fell on the apricot village
And grew into lines of apricot trees around the village.
The apricot flowers were smeared with rouge, eagerly awaiting to
 bloom.
The seed of the Waking of Insects fell into the peach valley,
And grew into 100 miles of peach forest.
As the spring drew on, the sweet smelling of peach flowers
 were everywhere.
The seed of the Vernal Equinox fell on the hills of my hometown
And grew into pear trees all over the mountains and plains.
White pear flowers were rippling with the wind like waves.
The seed of the Pure Brightness fell on both banks of the river
And grew into two rows of crooked willows.
The willow flowers were swinging and the air was full of fragrance.
The seed of the Grain Rain fell in the peony garden
And grew into a cluster of beautiful blossoms with divine fragrance.
They were blooming while the butterflies and bees were playing.

娇嗔的春天说还缺一粒种子
我的心里发了慌
种子落在了我的心坎上
情窦初开，没法讲

2017.4.13

Pretending to be angry, spring said that there was still another seed
    that was missing.
I panicked because
The seed had fallen into my heart
But I was in love and I could not speak.

April 13, 2017

羞涩春天

太阳暖暖，风儿淡淡
你低下头，站在面前
温柔了湖水，波光潋滟
乌黑的长辫，拴住了懵懂的情缘
纤细的嫩手，把发梢紧紧绕缠
红红的小嘴，轻轻咬住了春天
瞅瞅裙摆，看看脚尖
不敢抬头，对视一眼
春风把舌头打了卷
说不出心中爱的诺言
一抹绯红
把整个春天渲染

2017.4.11

Shy Spring

The sun is warm and the wind is light.
You bow your head and stand in front of me.
The gentle water of the lake is glittering.
Your long black braids are tied to ignorant love.
Your slender hands tightly twist the end of your long hair.
Your lovely red mouth gently holds the spring.
You look at your skirt then at the tips of your toes.
You are too shy to raise your head for a glance.
Your tongue is tied up by the spring breeze
So you are unable to tell me the promise of love in heart.
A touch of crimson
Decorates the whole spring.

April 11, 2017

等　你

扯一缕春风，等你
系在湖边的垂柳上
燕子却把春风丢在湖里
溅起淡淡的涟漪

捧一把春雨，等你
春雨却从指缝里悄悄溜走
不知落入谁的心底
留下一片湿润在梦里

捡一片花瓣，等你
十里桃花却迷失了自己
晶莹的露珠在晨曦里滑落
跌碎在往事里

2017.3.24

Waiting for You

I pull a wisp of spring wind, waiting for you,
And tie it to the weeping willow by the lake,
But the swallow throws the spring breeze into the lake
Making slight ripples.

I hold a handful of spring rain, waiting for you,
But the spring rain slips through my fingers quietly.
Whose heart does the spring rain fall into,
Leaving part of my dream moist.

I pick up a petal, waiting for you,
But I lose myself in the peach blossoms.
My tears fall in the morning,
Breaking into pieces in the memory.

March 24, 2017

初　恋

初恋，是一首朦胧诗
纯纯的爱，浓浓的情
描绘出一道美丽的彩虹

初恋，是一滴泪水
流过青春的面颊
品尝幸福和苦涩

初恋，是一抹春色
涂抹在了心底某个角落
不经意把黑夜浸润成玫瑰的颜色

2018.12.28

First Love

First love is a misty poem
Which is too pure and deep,
Painting a beautiful rainbow.

First love is a tear drop
Which flows on the cheek of the youth
Causing him to taste happiness and bitterness.

First love is a touch of spring
Which is painted at somewhere in the heart,
Soaking the black night into rosiness inadvertently.

December 28, 2018

一见钟情

知道，今生你我

来去匆匆

我在干涸的土地上

种上春风

等待将来某一天

与你一见钟情

当山谷里的花儿

笑盈盈

那一定是你派出的花童

通知我出来相迎

我张开双臂

薰衣草的花海里

把你深情相拥

亲吻你无尽的柔情

大声向春天宣布

一生与你同行

2017.2.28

Love at First Sight

I know that you and I
Come and go in a hurry this life.
In the arid land,
I plant spring breeze,
Waiting to fall in love with you at first sight.
When the flowers in the valley smile,
It must be the flower girl you dispatched,
Telling me to come out to meet you.
I open my arms,
In the sea of lavender flowers.
I lovingly hug you
And kiss you with endless tenderness.
I promise to spring loudly
That I'll love you all my life.

February 28, 2017

柳条弯弯

柳条弯弯
折一条做成花环
戴在你头上
衬托你美丽的笑脸
套住你我注定的姻缘
手拉手去追逐春天
人生苦短
爱情从来不晚
为了等你
我在上帝面前
已祈祷了三百年

2018.10.5

Bent Wicker

The wicker is bent
So I bent it to make a garland
And then put it on your head
To set off your beautiful smiling face.
We tie the knot
As we chase spring hand in hand.
Though life is too short,
It's never too late to fall in love.
In order to wait for you,
I have prayed to God
For 300 years.

October 5, 2018

欣 赏

黑夜里
我用执着的犁铧
耕耘缘分的天地
偷偷种下爱的太阳
每天早上等你
等你打开花窗
等太阳爬过山冈
把你美丽容颜照亮
我悄悄躲在太阳后边
把你欣赏

2016.7.31

Enjoying

In the dark night
I use the ploughshare of persistence
To cultivate the field of destiny
And secretly plant the sun of love.
I wait for you every morning,
Waiting for you to open the window,
Waiting for the sun to climb the hill
To light up your beautiful face.
I hide behind the sun quietly,
Enjoying you.

July 31, 2016

拥　抱

努力闭着双眼，不想睁开
怕世俗的目光，把我射穿
躲在你怀里，是我一生的期盼
仁慈的上帝啊，求你网开一面
让我俩就这样下去，相拥相恋
春风，把我俩紧紧缠绕
夏日的彩虹，为我俩打伞
秋天的枫叶，飘落在我俩的双肩
冬日的雪花，围绕我俩飞舞缠绵
直到我俩，凝固成大河边的岩石
看大江东去，彩霞满天
岁月的沧桑，无法模糊你我过去的斑斓
一遍一遍，清晰重现
时光的流水，无情冲刷着我俩的肢体
一点一点，消失不见
没有痛苦，没有遗憾
我俩的爱情，定格成永远

2018.10.24

Embrace

I try to keep my eyes closed and don't want to open them

Because I'm afraid the worldly eyes will see through me.

Hiding in your arms is the hope of my life.

Merciful God, please allow us

To go on like this, embracing and loving each other.

The spring breeze ties us tightly.

The summer rainbow holds an umbrella for us.

The autumn's maple leaves fall on our shoulders.

The snowflakes of winter swirl around us.

Until we solidify into the rock by the river,

Seeing the great river flowing east

And the sky full of rosy clouds.

The vicissitudes of time can not obscure our brightly colored past

Which comes to mind again and again.

The running water of time cleans our bodies

Which fade away little by little.

No pain, no regret.

Our love is fixed forever.

October 24, 2018

垂　柳

我是河边的一棵垂柳
在你面前我总是习惯低头
没有任何理由

你是一缕春风
轻轻拉住了我的手
给我披上一身翠绿
还你万条温柔

你是一只燕子
候着春天的理由
在我温暖的怀抱里
呢喃着来去自由

你是一条小鱼
在我眼前欢快畅游
我用美丽的倒影
衬托着你的自由

我是河边的一棵垂柳
冬天来临你却远走
寒风里我依然守候
对着你离去的方向翘首

2018.10.2

Weeping Willow

I am a weeping willow by the river.
I'm used to lowering my head in front of you
For no reasons.

You are a breath of spring breeze,
Gently holding my hands.
You dress me in jade green.
I give you all of my love in return.

You are a swallow,
Waiting for a sign of spring.
In my warm embrace,
You are free to come and go, chirping.

You are a little fish,
Swimming happily before my eyes.
My beautiful reflection
Always accompanies you

I am a weeping willow by the river.
When winter comes, you go far away.
I'm still waiting in the cold wind,
Looking longingly in the direction you went.

October 2, 2018

春

春风，吹开了花朵

融化了冷艳

清澈的溪水

流进褶皱的峡谷

把惊蛰的蝴蝶轻轻召唤

蝴蝶扑棱着美丽的翅膀

惊起春色一片

把两边峭壁浸染

我小心翼翼

不敢轻易上前

躲在入口旁垂涎

派出布谷鸟打探

却消失在无尽的深渊

我只好闭上双眼摸索向前

香草味弥漫双肩

耳畔是恣意的娇喘

原始的野性被点燃

纵横驰骋

却冲不出春的包围圈

醒来，已被埋葬在花海里边

春来了，怎敢怠慢

爱情之花，不会偷懒

春里盛开，春里娇艳

2018.7.23

Spring

The spring breeze caressed the flower
Thawing your cool beautiful body.
The clear stream
Flew into your plicated canyon,
Gently summoning the butterfly.
The butterfly flapped its beautiful wings
And gave a jolt to spring
Which colored the cliffs on both sides.
I was careful
And afraid to step forward,
Hiding near the entrance and drooling.
I sent out my cuckoo to scout
But it disappeared into the endless abyss.
I had to close my eyes, groping forward.
The smell of vanilla filled the air over my shoulders
And I heard the gasp of love.
My primitive wildness was ignited.
And I ran around
But couldn't get out of spring.
When I woke up, I found I was buried in a sea of flowers.
Spring has come, how can I neglect it?
The flower of love will never be lazy
And it is tender and beautiful, blooming in spring.

July 23, 2018

红　酒

迷离的灯光下，轻盈把盏
萨克斯有一搭无一搭地吹着秋天
猩红色旋转，一抹窈窕柔绵
浓郁的液体，滑过鲜红的嘴边
品不完的味道，呷不尽的无言
暧昧的酒色，性感的夜晚
泛红的面颊，惺忪的双眼
醉人的媚态，无法遮掩
飘飘欲仙，怎能忘记昨夜的缠绵
几滴相思泪，渲染了寂寞从前
几分眩晕，几分梦幻
几分回忆，几分伤感
多一分高雅，多一分浪漫
多一分风韵，多一分性感
红酒懂女人，相知无言
女人，是红酒灵魂的代言
女人梦，在红酒里斑斓
红酒，让女人散发出迷人的气息
熏醉了记忆，忘记了时间
璀璨的霓虹灯，正在华丽上演
懂红酒的儒雅男人，还未出现
不眠之夜，谁是解开我风情的红颜

2018.9.26

Red Wine

Under the dim light, I lightly hold the glass
With the saxophone playing autumn music.
I spin the glass slowly and the red wine is thick.
The red liquid slides into my mouth from my red lips.
But it doesn't have a flavor, so I keep silent.
The color of red wine is inexplicit and the night is sexy.
My cheeks are red and my eyes are sleepy.
I can't cover up my intoxicating coquetry.
I'm drunk, but I can't forget yesterday's love.
A few tear drops prove my lonely past.
Am I a little dizzy or dreamy?
Am I a little reminiscent or sentimental?
I want to be much nobler and more romantic.
I want to be more charming and much sexier.
Red wine knows a woman, but it has no words.
A woman is the spokesperson of the red wine's soul.
Red wine makes a woman's dream romantic.
Red wine causes a woman to give off an enchanting smell
Which makes her memory drunk and forget the time.
The neon lights are bright tonight
But a refined man who understands red wine hasn't appeared.
In this white night, who can know my amorous feelings?

September 26, 2018

如果我爱你

如果我爱你，第一次见面
我不会送你玫瑰花
它是蔷薇物种杂交和回交形成的
并不代表纯洁

如果我爱你，你过生日时
我不会送你巧克力
它并不只有甜蜜
对马和狗等动物来说它是毒药

如果我爱你，哄你时
我不会向着月亮发誓
月亮是靠太阳发光的
并不代表我的心

如果我爱你，你嫁给我时
我不会给你戴上钻戒
它不象征永恒
用火烧，它就没了

如果我爱你，婚后
我不会比喻我俩是鸳鸯鸟
鸳鸯每次相拥的都是不同的伴侣
是个典型的花心大萝卜

If I Love You

If I love you,

I will not give you a rose when we meet for the first time.

It is a rose specie formed by crossbreeding and backcrossing,

So it is not at all pure.

If I love you,

I will not give you chocolate on your birthday.

It's not only sweet

But also poisonous to animals such as horses and dogs.

If I love you,

I will not swear to the moon when I try to make you happy.

It is illuminated by the sun,

So it does not represent my heart.

If I love you,

I will not put a diamond ring on your finger on our wedding.

If you burn it, it will be gone,

So it does not symbolize eternity.

If I love you,

I will not liken us to lovebirds after we're married.

A lovebird's partner is different each time,

So it is a typical playboy.

如果我爱你，今生
我会把一切给你
让时间来验证承诺
用生命演绎爱情奇迹

2018.9.22

If I love you,

I will give you all that I own in this life.

Let time verify my promise to you

And use this life to unfold the miracle of love.

September 22, 2018

江 河

我俩是两条不同的河流
你是南方奔腾的大江
我是北方涓涓的小河
你宽阔的胸怀气势磅礴
我潺潺的溪水自由漂泊
你冲刷掉岁月无情的痕迹
我洗涤出时光无言的底色
崇山峻岭将你我远远阻隔
你我无法冲破这千山万壑
知道生命的里程中没有交汇
我俩只好遥遥相望，祝福默默
我懂你汛期波涛汹涌的诉说
你了解我冬季千里冰封的寂寞
因为我俩都有奔向东方的执着
生命的终点我俩将会融合
浩渺的太平洋是我俩永恒爱的寄托

2018.8.10

Rivers

We are two different rivers.

You are the great surging river of the south

While I'm the trickling brook of the north.

Your open mind is magnificent

And my stream runs freely.

You wash out the ruthless traces of time

And I wash clean the silent background of time.

The steep mountains keep us far apart.

We can't break through the barriers of mountains.

We know there is no meeting in the journey of lives

And we can only face each other from far, blessing silently.

I know your excited telling in the flood season

And you understand my icebound loneliness in winter.

As we both persist to run toward the east.

At the end of our lives we will meet and merge

Because our everlasting love is hiding in the vast Pacific Ocean.

August 10, 2018

胡　须

分别后的日子
胡须，疯长
沧桑了往日
你温柔的模样
远方的你
是否找到了
心仪的人儿
希望，他的胡须
和我的一样长

2016.7.15

Beard

After our separation
My beard has grown insanely long,
Obscuring your past tenderness.
I wonder if you have a new lover
In the distance.
I hope his beard
Is as long as mine.

July 15, 2016

雨,还在下

雨水,滴答
在玻璃上,画着流动的窗花
你别来,路太滑
一个人,我不怕
别牵挂,你送给我的狗
望着我,不说话
煮一杯蓝山咖啡
听一曲你喜欢的音乐
看一遍你写的微信情话
雨,还在下

2017.8.16

It Is Still Raining

Rain is falling from the sky,

Drawing pictures on the window.

Don't come out because the road is too slippery.

I'm alone but I am not scared.

Don't worry about me

And the dog you gave me

Is looking at me, saying nothing.

I'm making a cup of Blue Mountain Coffee,

Listening to the soft music you like

And reading your love poems on WeChat

Since it is still raining.

August 16, 2017

今晚我是你的新娘

黑夜里，用思念
点燃忧伤，把房间照亮
穿上你为我买的美丽衣裳
你曾说，我身上有星星
眼睛像月亮
今晚，我就是你的新娘
等你，把门铃摁响
抱我上床，慢慢欣赏

2016.3.12

Tonight, I'm Your Bride

At night, I use my longing

To set fire to the sorrow to light up the room

And put on the beautiful clothes you bought for me.

You said that the stars are on my body

And my eyes are like the moon.

Tonight, I am your bride.

I'm waiting for you to ring the doorbell.

Then carry me to bed and slowly enjoy watching me.

March 12, 2016

贪婪

流连，秘密的花园
那里有，满目的春天
春雨滋润了，粗糙的从前
青春的枝头，在里边尽情舒展
一朵朵玉兰花，恣意绽放着爱的缠绵
春色，让人变得越来越贪婪

2016.3.12

Greed

I'm reluctant to leave,
Lingering in your secret garden
Which is full of spring.
Spring rain moistens my rough past.
My young branches stretch widely.
Magnolia flowers are recklessly blooming.
Spring makes me greedier and greedier.

March 12, 2016

相思钱

你是我，一生的期盼
我却是你，偶尔路过的酒馆
你享用了我，珍藏了一世的缠绵
留给我，残羹冷炙的孤单
没付我丁点，相思的钱
因为愿意，我不遗憾

2016.12.12

Money of Lovesickness

You are my lifelong expectation
While I'm only the pub which you pass by occasionally.
You have enjoyed my love that I have treasured up all my life,
Leaving me the leftovers of loneliness
Without even paying me a little money of lovesickness.
Because I am willing to do this, I have no regrets.

December 12, 2016

爱与性

爱，像一个盲人
没有方向
一路跌跌撞撞
性，是一种生理现象
拥抱着孤独
黑夜里遥望
爱是性的调味品
性是爱的最好奖赏
爱不是性偶尔路过的客房
性更不是爱的救世主
相爱的人依然会忧伤
离别的人总是痛苦彷徨
如果寂寞与性有关
为何爱总让人痴狂
阳光透过人生的缝隙
把性的孤独照亮
性和爱手拉手
快乐走在大街上
一起看爱情的太阳

2018.7.27

Love and Sex

Love is like a blind man

Who has no direction,

Staggering all the way.

Sex is a physiological phenomenon,

Embracing loneliness

And looking in the distance at night.

Love is the spice of sex

And sex is the best reward for love.

Love is not a guest room which sex passes by occasionally

And sex is not the savior of love.

Those who love each other will still be sad.

Those who break up are always hurt and perplexed.

If loneliness is related to sex,

Why does love always make people crazy?

Light shines through the cracks of life,

Lighting loneliness up in life.

Sex and love walk hand in hand,

Happily walking down the street

And watching the sun of love together.

July 27, 2018

爱情长城

你住长城北

我住长城南

独自登上长城

把往事游览

汗水迷了双眼

你温柔的爱

激励我奋力登攀

站在好汉坡

才能向着远方的你发誓

邂逅的缘分

让我触摸到爱情的云端

厚重的历史

孕育爱情的新鲜

孟姜女的哭泣声

隐约在耳边

爱情的悲剧

不会在你我之间重演

长城就像我对你的思念

翻山越岭，蜿蜒不断

长城就像我对你的爱

默默无言，亘古永远

2018.7.19

The Great Wall of Love

You live north of the Great Wall
While I live in south of it.
I climb the Great Wall alone,
Reviewing the past.
My eyes are blinded by sweats
But your tender love
Is inspiring me to climb
Because only when standing at the Bawcock Slope
Can I pledge to you in the distance.
The destiny of our unexpected meeting
Lets me touch true love.
The rich history
Makes our love fresh.
I hear faintly
Meng Jiangnu crying.
The tragedy of love
Will not happen again between us.
The Great Wall is like my yearning for you
Which windingly covers the mountains.
The Great Wall is like my love to you,
Silent and eternal.

July 19, 2018

爱情密码

家乡的小溪，弯弯
清澈的溪水，潺潺
她，追逐着蝴蝶
嬉戏右岸，花枝招展
他，沐浴着春风
漫步左岸，风度翩翩
相对一视，似相识多年
石击心源，涟漪泛滥
她羞怯呢喃，告诉脚下的花儿
他是她千年的梦幻
他神魂摇曳，告诉旁边的小溪
她是他万年的期盼
相遇是缘，不早不晚
不约而同，顺着小溪向前
前方，有座小桥
他俩可以相会，手相牵
爱情密码，已暴露给了春天

2018.6.30

The Code of Love

There was a winding brook in my hometown

Which was clear and gurgling.

A gorgeously dressed girl was frolicking,

Chasing butterflies on the right bank.

A handsome and elegant boy

Was wandering on the left bank.

When they were looking at each other,

It seemed that they'd known each other for many years,

Which was like a stone thrown into the lake of the heart,

Stirring so much rippling.

She was shy and timid, whispering to the flower at her feet

That he was her long time dream.

He was obsessed with her, telling the brook nearby

That she was his long time hope.

Meeting was a destiny and it came on time.

They followed the brook simultaneously.

There was a small bridge ahead,

Where they could meet and hold hands.

The code of love had been revealed to spring.

June 30, 2018

女人的爱情

女人的爱情
像美丽的粽子
层层粽叶
包裹着丰满的情感
第一层是焦虑
"你喜欢我吗？"
第二层是求证
"你爱我吗？"
第三层是落实
"什么时候结婚？"
女人喜欢递增
男人喜欢递减
等拨开最后一层粽叶
他的眼眶湿润了
一个晶莹剔透的粽子
那是女人的爱情
紧致密实的糯米
如同女人缜密的心思
告诉我，心仪的人啊
何时脱掉我的衣衫
让我粽香泛滥
甜在你的心尖
给你我最好的端午浪漫

2018.6.18

Woman's Love

A woman's love

Is like a beautiful rice dumpling

In which the fullness of love is wrapped

With layers of indocalamus leaves.

The first layer is anxiety:

"Do you like me?"

The second one is seeking confirmation:

"Do you love me?"

The third one is practical:

"When will we get married?"

The woman likes to play hard-to-get

While the man loves to get straightway.

When he finally removes the last layer of indocalamus leaves,

He is moved to tears

Because he sees the crystal-like rice dumpling

Which is the woman's love.

Tightly packed glutinous rice

Is like a woman's meticulous mind.

Tell me, my sweetheart,

When will you take off my clothes,

And let me give off the fragrance of rice dumplings

And sweetness in heart?

This will be the most romantic Dragon Boat Festival I can give you

June 18, 2018

给我生个孩子吧

与你相识，命中注定
你的歌声里，有我爱的憧憬
不想影响你，灿烂的前程
不能许你，花前月下
也许放手，才是该有的清醒
你单纯的心中，藏着执着的爱情
给我力量，让我与你再次重逢
世间最美的结局，是和你相伴终身
我再也不会，离你远行
不想解释，别人不懂
相爱，是最好的说明
情不知所起，一往情深
爱情一旦深入心，就永远如影随形
你嫁给爱情，我为爱情而生
彼此相懂，就是最好的人生
年龄差距，我不能陪你全程
祈求你，嫁给我
给我生个孩子吧，像我一样
我不在了，他替我把你疼

2018.6.12

Give Me a child

It's fate to meet you.

My love is hiding in your singing

Because I don't want to affect your bright future.

I can't walk by the flowers and under the moon with you,

So perhaps letting go is the right thing to do.

In your pure heart there is persistent love

Which gives me the strength to meet you again.

The most beautiful ending in the world

Is to be with you for the rest of my life

And I will never leave you again.

We needn't explain because others can't understand

And love is the best indication.

I don't know when I began to love you

But I continue to love you more and more.

Once love walks into the heart,

It will never walk out.

You marry me for love and I live with you for love.

Knowing each other is the best thing in life.

I can't accompany you all the life

Because I'm much older than you,

So I beg you to marry me

And give me a child who is like me.

After I die, he will love you more deeply than me.

June 12, 2018

火　种

你的眼里
有春天，浪漫
我想躲进去
花枝招展

你的连衣裙里
有夏天，性感
我想钻进去
和你缠绵

你的胸脯上
有秋天，丰满
我想吸吮
生命的源泉

你对我的态度里
有冬天，冷淡
我想变成火种
把爱情重新点燃

2018.6.3

Kindling

Inside your eyes is
A romantic spring.
I want to hide in them,
Dressing colorfully.

Inside your dress is
A sexy summer.
I want to get inside and
Make love with you.

Inside your chest is
A plump autumn
I want to drink
From the well-spring of life.

Inside your attitude toward me is
A cold winter.
I want to be the spark
That rekindles our love.

June 3, 2018

爱情的童心

爱情的童心
是清晨第一缕阳光
水灵灵，亮晶晶
跳跃在你跟前
望着你，真高兴
像一个五彩斑斓的梦

爱情的童心
是天上无数的星星
带着天真的幻想
朝你眨眼睛
你永远不知道
什么时候她会进入你梦中

爱情的童心
是一个喜欢捉迷藏的孩子
藏在初恋的梦里
藏在热恋的卿卿我我中
藏在婚姻中的奋斗里
藏在老年相依相偎的笑容里

爱情的童心
是幸福树上的花朵
春色里自由绽放

Childlike Innocence of Love

The childlike innocence of love
Is like the first ray of sunshine in the early morning.
It's beautiful and glittering.
Dancing in front of you,
She is looking at you happily
Like a colorful dream.

The childlike innocence of love
Is like the countless stars in the sky.
She is blinking towards you
With a naive fantasy,
But you will never know
When she will go into your dream.

The childlike innocence of love
Is like child who likes playing hide-and-seek,
Hiding in the dream of the first love,
Hiding in the lovey-dovey feelings of the passionate love,
Hiding in the struggle of the marriage
And hiding in the smile of the interdependent later years.

The childlike innocence of love
Is like the flower on a happy tree,
Blooming freely in spring.

蜜蜂围绕她来回飞行
爱情的真正意义
在于快乐永恒

2018.5.31

The bees are flying all around her.

The true meaning of love

Is to be happy forever.

May 31 , 2018

撩　拨

你不必撩拨我
不远万里来的情人
我是你脚下的湖水
正等待着你脚丫亲吻
荡起悠悠涟漪波纹

你不必撩拨我
不远万里来的情人
我是湖边小屋里的琴
不管你轻抚哪根琴弦
都会弹奏出我起伏的呻吟

你不必撩拨我
不远万里来的情人
今晚我是你的人
湖水已溢出我的心
你永远不知道湖水有多深

2018.5.29

Tantalizing

My lover, you need not tantalize me
Though you have traveled tens of thousands of miles.
I am the lake water under your feet,
Waiting for your feet to kiss me
And to ripple the water gently.

My lover, you need not tantalize me
Though you have traveled tens of thousands of miles.
I'm the piano in the lakeside cottage.
No matter which key you put down,
You can play my various chords easily.

My lover, you need not tantalize me
Though you have traveled tens of thousands of miles.
I am yours tonight.
The lake water is overflowing from my heart
And you will never know how deep is is.

May 29, 2018

爱总走在左边

爱，总走在左边
不紧不慢
性，老走在右边
拖拽着我的衣衫
我的灵魂为你躲闪
不希望原始的性
蹂躏了我俩爱的香甜
其实，爱情和性
一直是好伙伴
性是一种本能的冲动
爱有时会被性欺骗
性是赤裸天真
爱是复杂的情感
身体没有谎言
爱是性的源泉
性是人性的使然
灵魂不迁就性的泛
爱只有长出蓓蕾
性之花才能开得灿烂
爱是导航
指引着性勇往直前
爱和性，少了谁
人生都是遗憾
爱要优先

Love Always Walks on the Left

Love always walks on the left,
Slowly and unhurriedly.
Sex always walks on the right,
Dragging my clothes.
My soul is dodging because of you.
I don't want our desire
To override the sweetness of our love.
In fact, love and sex
Are always good partners.
Sex is an instinctive impulse.
And sometimes love is deceived by sex.
Sex is a naked innocence
But love is a complex emotion.
The body never tells a lie
And love is the source of sex.
Sex is the cause of human nature
But the soul doesn't indulge in sexual excesses.
Only when a bud grows from love,
Can the flower of sex bloom brilliantly.
Love is a navigator,
Guiding sex to go forward bravely.
It is a pity for us
To lack love or sex.
Give priority to love

没有爱的性
我宁愿孤单
爱你性感的躯体
更爱你灵魂的丰满

2018.5.18

And if my sex lacks love,

I would rather be alone.

I love your sexy body

But I love the fullness of your soul more.

May 18, 2018

缘

相遇，是缘
你情，我愿
今生，没遗憾
即使，你离开
我也不会纠缠
因为，你已经
把温柔留给了春风
把热情留给了夏日
把缠绵留给了秋雨
把思念留给了冬夜
四季轮回，其实
你一直在我身边

2018.5.17

Destiny

Meeting you is our destiny

Because we fell in love with each other.

I will never regret in my life.

Even if you leave me,

I will not pester you

Because you have already

Left your tenderness in the spring breeze,

Left your enthusiasm in summer,

Left your lingering love in the autumn rain,

And left your thoughts feelings in the winter night.

Actually, in the cycle of seasons,

You are continually with me.

May 17, 2018

我　愿

我愿是一条小河
在你初恋的记忆里
悠悠流淌

我愿是一片雪花
在你相思的梦里
悄悄飘落

我愿是一棵小草
在你生活的缝隙里
丰盈生长

我愿是一朵花
在你春天般的怀抱里
默默盛开

我愿是一支笛子
在你茫茫的思想原野上
笛声悠扬

我愿是一艘巨轮
在你大海般的胸怀里
缓缓前行

2018.5.16

I Wish

I wish I were a creek,
Flowing slowly
In the memory of your first love.

I wish I were a piece of snowflake,
Falling quietly
In your dream of lovesickness.

I wish I were a blade of grass,
Growing plumply
In the crevice of your life.

I wish I were a flower,
Blooming silently
In your youthful arms.

I wish I were a flute,
Whistling melodiously
In the wilderness of your thoughts.

I wish I were a giant ship,
Moving slowly
In the sea of your mind.

May 16, 2018

今晚，月食

夜色，属于他和她
孤独的萤火虫
荒野里，跳舞
欲望猫，躲在角落里
睁大了贪婪的眼
原始的野性，碰撞
击碎了温柔的梦境
一声孤狼最后的低吼，惊起
灵魂，离开了美丽的躯体
她是月亮，他是太阳
看不见他的脸
今晚，月食

2018.5.15

There Is an Eclipse Tonight

Darkness belonged to him and her.

The lonely firefly

Was dancing in the wilderness.

The eager cat was hiding in the corner,

Opening its greedy eyes.

Her tender dream was shattered

By the burning desire.

When the lone wolf growled at last, she was shocked

And her soul left from her beautiful body.

She's the moon and he's the sun

But she can't see his face.

There is an eclipse tonight.

May 15, 2018

爱　河

你站在爱河的东边
我站在爱河的西岸
你那边朝霞漫天
我这边日薄西山
你美丽的脸
像早晨的玫瑰
我疲惫的眼里
长河落日圆
假如我向东迈一步
就站在了爱河边
再向东迈一步
就掉入爱河
假如你向西迈一步
就站在了爱河边
再向西迈一步
我俩就都掉进爱河
一起顺流向前

2018.5.9

Love River

You're standing on the eastern side of the love river

While I'm standing on the western bank.

The sky is filled with morning glows over your eastern bank

But the sun is setting over the western bank.

Your beautiful face

Is like the morning rose.

In my tired eyes,

The sun is setting

With the love river flowing in the distance.

If I take a step to the east,

I will stand next to the love river.

Taking a second step to the west,

I will fall into the love river.

If you take a step towards the east,

You will stand by the love river.

If you take a second step to the west,

We will both fall into the love river,

Floating downstream together.

May 9, 2018

蓝月亮

一直，走在悬崖边
摇摇晃晃，只为等待
梦里，蓝月亮的出现
茫茫大海，望不到边
脚下，万丈深渊
手拉手，依然坚定向前
相信，蓝月亮不是美丽的谎言
终于，蓝月亮冒出了海平面
那么美丽，那么遥远
翘足，伸手去摘
失去平衡，他俩滑向深渊
紧紧拥抱，不再孤单
一起下落，心甘情愿
漂浮在月光中
那么轻，落得那么慢
天上的蓝月亮在长
海里的蓝月亮在晃
她问，哪一个蓝月亮更圆
他说，最圆的在心里边
不要害怕，不要忧伤
大海会把思念永藏
死亡是爱情圆满的寿衣裳

2018.5.7

Blue Moon

They always walked on the edge of a cliff,

Staggering, only waiting for

The blue moon to appear in the dream.

The sea was too vast to see the edge.

And at the foot was the abyss

But they still walked forward firmly, hand in hand.

They didn't believe the blue moon was a beautiful white lie.

Finally, the blue moon rose above the sea level,

So beautiful and far away.

They tried to pick the blue moon on ther tiptoes.

But they lost their balance and slid down into the abyss.

Hugging tightly, they would never feel lonely.

They were willing to fall together.

Floating in the moonlight,

They fell slowly and lightly.

The blue moon in the sky was rising

And the moon in the sea was shaking.

She asked which blue moon was much rounder.

He said the roundest one was in their hearts.

Don't be afraid and don't be sad.

The sea will hide your longing forever.

Death is love's perfect shroud.

May 7, 2018

吻

吻，吻啊吻
吻得春天羞涩地闭上了眼
两座挺立的山峰顶上，红晕弥漫
冰雪融化，泉水潺潺

吻，吻啊吻
吻得夏日狂风雷电
江河痉挛，淹没了所有
留下短暂漆黑一片

吻，吻啊吻
吻得秋天满山红遍
果实丰满，秋水绵绵
簇拥着映入眼帘

吻，吻啊吻
吻得冬日忘掉了严寒
张着嘴巴像得了哮喘
呼吸融化了雪花片片

2018.5.6

Kiss

Kiss, kiss and kiss,
Kissing spring's shyly closed eyes.
The two mountain peaks are completely covered in red.
The ice is melting and the spring water is rippling.

Kiss, kiss and kiss,
Kissing summer's wind and storms.
The rivers are convulsing, drowning everything.
Only a moment of darkness is left.

Kiss, kiss and kiss,
Kissing autumn's red mountains.
The fruits are ample and the water is continually flowing,
As far as the eyes can see.

Kiss, kiss and kiss,
Kissing winter to forget the bitter cold.
Opening the mouth is like having an asthma attack.
Each breath melts the snowflakes.

May 6, 2018

渴　望

多么渴望，变成一缕春风
抚平你脸上的沧桑
亲吻你的单纯和善良

多么渴望，做一棵大树
让你夏日里好乘凉
听恋曲在耳旁悠扬

多么渴望，变成一只宠物犬
你回家后和你做伴
排遣你的孤单

多么渴望，变成一张大床
你夜里舒服地躺在上面
甜甜进入梦乡

多么渴望，变成广阔的蓝天
你可以展开浪漫的翅膀
自由飞翔

多么渴望，摘下你的面具
露出你娇柔的鲜花模样
让我仔细欣赏

2018.5.4

Wishes

I wish I could become a gust of spring breeze
To smooth out the vicissitudes of life on your face,
Kissing your purity and goodness.

I wish I could become a tall tree
So I could keep you cool in the summer
While you listen to love songs.

I wish I could become a pet dog
Who will accompany you when you get home,
Diverting yourself from loneliness

I wish I could become a big bed
In which you can lie on comfortably at night
And fall asleep soundly.

I wish I could become the vast blue sky
In which you can spread your romantic wings
And fly freely.

I wish I could take off your mask,
Revealing your tender looks.
So I can enjoy you carefully.

May 4, 2018

我爱你

你在海的另一边
无法给你，我的温暖
我愿变成一滴海水
随着思念的洋流
勇敢漂荡向前
看漫天星斗翻转
观海天一色壮观
潜入漆黑的海底
感受大海无边的寂寞
冲进滔天巨浪
聆听大海委屈的诉说
你是我今生的唯一
漂洋过海不是距离
一定有一天我会漂流到你面前
当你戏水时，轻轻亲吻你的脚面
即使你走上沙滩
把我抖落在沙子里
我也要化作一丝气体
钻进你的鼻孔
进入你的肺里
融化在你的血液里
再也不离开你
因为，我爱你

2018.4.28

I Love You

You are on the other side of the sea
And I can't keep you warm.
I'd like to be a drop of seawater
Which moves forward bravely
With the ocean current of longing.
I'll gaze at the falling stars
And watch the spectacular sight.
The sea and sky merge into one.
I'll dive into the dark seabed,
And feel the endless loneliness of the sea.
I'll rush into the monstrous billows
And listen to the sea pouring out her grievances.
You are the only one in my life
And it isn't a long distance to cross the sea.
There will be a day when I am in front of you.
When you paddle, I'll gently kiss on your feet.
Even if you walk on the sandy beach,
Shaking me off in the sand,
I'll change into a hint of gas,
Running into your nostrils,
Entering your lungs
And melting in your blood.
I will never leave you again
Because I love you.

April 28, 2018

爱情春天

冬天总是走得蹒跚
倒春寒不时在记忆里流连
爱情的种子已埋在了心间
怎能错过一年一次的春天
不在角落里安静地睡眠
十里桃花催我踏青走向前

如果你视而不见
我会变成一缕春风
悄悄躲在你耳后边
聆听爱情之花盛开的誓言
或者变成一只美丽的花蝴蝶
轻轻飘落在你俊俏的双肩
与你的秀发争奇斗艳
或者变成小路旁的一株小草
欣赏你一路走来花枝招展
等你偶尔停下脚步，俯身抚摸我的脸

如果你羞涩地垂下眼帘
我就用春风为你折一个风车
在你丰腴温暖的怀抱里
幸福地亲吻旋转
或者用春雨撑一把小伞
相思泪滴滑落在你的花裙边

Spring of Love

Winter always leaves late.
A cold spell in late spring often lingers in my memory.
The seed of love has been buried in my heart.
Spring happens once a year, so I cannot miss it.
I can not sleep quietly in the corner any longer
And ten miles of peach blossoms urge me to go ahead.

If you turn a blind eye,
I will become a wisp of spring breeze
And hide behind your ears,
Listening to the vows of love in full bloom.
Or I will turn into a beautiful butterfly,
Gently fluttering on your elegant shoulders
And contending with your beautiful hair.
Or I will become a little blade of grass by the side of the road
And enjoy you walking in your beautiful dress,
Waiting for you to occasionally stop and lean over to caress my face.

If you bashfully close your eyes,
I will use the spring breeze to make a windmill for you
To kiss you and spin happily
In your plump and warm embrace.
Or I will use the spring rain to open an umbrella
And my tears of lovesickness fall on your flowery skirt,

滋养初恋爱情的春天
或者用春天的眼睛为你拍照
留下你无尽的温柔和缠绵
寒冬里围在火炉旁，一起回忆从前

草长莺飞中漫步垂柳河边
心仪的人儿一定藏在春天
姹紫嫣红把春色渲染
我却分不清哪是花哪是你的笑脸
亲爱的人啊，人间四月天
爱情来了，你可千万别躲闪

2018.3.3

Nourishing spring's first love.

Or I will take a picture of you with the eyes of spring

And leave you with endless tenderness and lingering emotion,

Recalling our past together around the stove in the cold winter.

The grass is growing and the birds are flying

And my lover—you must be hiding in spring.

The brilliant purple and red flowers bring out the colors of spring

But I can't tell which is the flower and which is your smiling face.

My dear lover, now it is April in the world.

When love comes, please do not hide.

March 3, 2018

记 忆

执一盏小灯
在长满青苔的记忆里
寻觅那飘零的情缘
静静滑过的泪水
灯下亮闪闪
也许年太少
也许相遇太早
时光模糊了你的容貌
思念为我画地为牢
你答应过我
回到我身旁
带着满身紫荆的清香
亲爱的人啊
请你告诉我
你已找到天堂

2018.2.23

Memory

Holding a small lamp

In my mossy memory,

I'm looking for fallen love.

My tears shone in the light

As they quietly ran down my cheeks.

Maybe we were too young

Or we met too early

Because time has blurred your looks

And my longing for you keeps me in prison.

You promised me

That you would come back

With the smell of sweet perfume.

My dearest,

Please tell me

You have found the paradise.

February 23, 2018

爱 情

以为你一定会回来
我一直在寂寞中等待
等待与你邂逅在音乐厅门外
等待与你奔跑在辽阔的大海边
等待与你深情拥吻在婚礼殿堂
等待年迈时与你携手漫步在夕阳中
可你却一直没有来
不知你为何要违背曾经许下的诺言
你说过我是你的缘
你说过我俩的爱情会永远

如果等待是模糊的记忆
为何深夜里你的名字那么清晰
如果等待是发黄的影集
为何你的笑容依然那么美丽
如果等待是那个熟悉的电话号码
为何每次拨打听到的都是无言
我只有独自徘徊在午夜的街头
等待岁月花开花落
等待无意中闻到你的气息
等待你悄悄走来给我一个惊喜

我也曾在鹊桥上漫步
等待你我像牛郎织女般每年相聚
我也曾像孟姜女一样在长城上恸哭

Love

I thought you would come back
So I've been waiting in solitude,
Waiting to meet you by chance outside the concert hall,
Waiting to run with you beside the vast sea,
Waiting to embrace and kiss you affectionately at the wedding hall,
Waiting to stroll with you hand in hand in the sunset,
But you haven't come yet.
I do not know why you break your promise
Since you said I was your destingy.
And you said that our love would last forever.

If waiting is a blurry memory,
Why is your name always clear in my mind at night?
If waiting is an old album,
Why is your smile still so beautiful?
If waiting is that familiar phone number,
Why do you always keep silent when I dial every time?
I only pace back and forth alone on the street at night,
Waiting for the flowers to bloom,
Waiting to unexpectedly smell your scent,
Waiting for you to come quietly and surprise me.

I have also walked on the Magpie Bridge,
Waiting to meet you there like Cowherd and Weaver Maid every year.
I have also wailed, crying like Meng Jiangnu on the Great Wall,

等待泪水能把阻隔我俩的世俗城墙哭倒
我也曾在梁祝同窗共烛的地方徘徊
等待一对彩蝶飞舞着把你引来
我也曾在美丽的西湖岸边踯躅
等待许仙和白娘子推着你向我走来
但你终究还是没有来

是时间苍白了等待
还是你输给了无奈
我问水塘边的鸳鸯
鸳鸯戏水默默离开
我问南国的红豆
红豆低头笑而不语
我问天山脚下的薰衣草
薰衣草在微风中摇摆
我问花园里的玫瑰
玫瑰花送来醉人的清香

早已习惯了等待
疲惫的我已不想离开
等待是一种幸福
等待是一种无奈
即使今生你不会再来
我也会在等待中默默走向未来
如果有一天我俩梦里相逢
我会紧紧抱住你
沉睡在你温暖的怀抱里
永不醒来

2018.1.30

148

Waiting for my tears to make the secular wall that separates us fall
   down.
I've also wandered in the place where Liang Shanbo and ZhuYingtai
   studied,
Waiting for a pair of butterflies to lead you to me.
I've also loitered around on the bank of the beautiful West Lake,
Waiting for Xu Xian and the Lady White Snake to push you towards me.
But you haven't come after all.

Is it time that has faded waiting
Or did you lose to the heplessness?
I asked the mandarin ducks by the pond,
But they paddled away quietly.
I asked the southern red beans
But they lowered their heads, laughing without words.
I asked the lavender at the foot of Tian Shan,
But they fluttered in the light breeze.
I asked the roses in the garden,
But they sent me an intoxicating fragrance.

I don't want to leave though I'm tired
Because I am used to waiting.
Waiting is a kind of happiness.
Waiting is a kind of helplessness.
Even though you will not come again,
I will also wait in silence for the future
If we meet in a dream one day,
I will hug you tightly,
Sleep in your warm arms
And never wake up.

January 30, 2018

冬 天

没有春天的花枝招展

也没有夏天的热火朝天

更没有秋天的多愁善感

你总是默默无言

晶莹剔透的肢体

卧在雪山草原

挂在故乡的屋檐

一只小狗静静趴在炉前

街灯下等待的是昨夜的孤单

思念的鸟儿已不再冬眠

惊起河边枯枝一片

唤醒了潜伏在骨髓里的灵魂

随着漫天的雪花舞翩跹

亲吻被冻结的泪水

从领口钻进温暖的胸前

拥抱梦里的水晶之恋

冬是春的序曲

爱的春天已经不远

2018.1.25

Winter

Without the blooming flowers of spring,

Without the vibrancy of summer,

Without the sentiment of autumn,

You are always silent.

Your crystal clear body

Is lying in the snow-covered mountains and grasslands,

Hanging from the cottage's eaves.

A puppy is quietly lying in front of the stove.

Last night's loneliness is waiting for you under the streetlights.

The bird of longing in my heart will not hibernate any longer,

Flying from the dead branches by the river.

The soul hidden in the bone marrow is awakened,

Dancing trippingly with snowflakes in the sky,

Kissing the frozen tears,

Slipping into the warm chest from the neckline

And hugging the crystal love in the dream.

Winter is the prelude to spring,

So the love of spring is not far.

January 25, 2018

一个人的旅行

厌倦生活的重复
逃离无奈的人情
芸芸众生里寂寥清醒
大千世界中独自旅行
如骏马一样在草原上驰骋
似吉卜赛人般流浪远行
欣赏无尽的美丽风景
寻找前方每一秒意想不到的感动
亲吻天边每一朵浪花
远眺地平线上旭日东升
朝霞里聆听乡间每一声鸟鸣
斜阳中看倦鸟归巢慰藉亲情
昆明的花海里有你的倩影
周庄古镇里与丁香一样的你相逢
亚得里亚海飘来你相思的歌声
夏威夷海滩上你性感的肢体迷住了我的眼睛
喜马拉雅雪山上埋藏着你春天的憧憬
呼伦贝尔草原上吹来你凉爽的风
贝加尔湖水滋润着你纯洁的心灵
尼亚加拉瀑布把你绘成一道绚丽的彩虹
亲爱的人啊，你一定在前方某个地方把我相迎
朝着你的方向，我风雨兼程
因为你那里，才有我最想看的风景

2018.1.22

Traveling Alone

I was tired of the repetition of life,

So I left the helpless human relationships.

Being lonely and sober in the midst of people,

I traveled alone in the world,

Galloping on the grasslands like a noble steed,

Wandering far from home like a gypsy,

Enjoying the endless beauty of the landscape

And looking forward to unexpected touches every second.

Kiss every spindrift in remote places.

Overlook the sun rising from the horizon.

Listen to the bird singing along the country road in the morning sunlight.

See the tired bird flying back to the nest to comfort its family.

Your shadow is in the sea of flowers in Kunming.

I meet you, the person like a lilac in the Zhouzhuang Ancient Town.

Your lovesick song is flying over the Adriatic Sea.

I'm captivated by your sexy body on the beach of Hawaii.

Your longing of spring is hidden under the snow of Himalayas.

Your cool wind is blowing from the Hulun Buir Prairie.

Your pure heart is moistened by the water of Baikal.

Niagara Falls draws you as a brilliant rainbow.

My lover, you must be waiting for me somewhere ahead.

In the wind and rain I go forward in your direction

Because only at the place where you are can I see the most beautiful scenery.

January 22, 2018

寻 你

你在哪里
我去村边的小树林里，寻你
那里曾是我俩小时玩耍的宝地
厚厚的白雪却覆盖了曾经的童趣
我去魂牵梦萦的母校，寻你
那里记载着我俩相约一生的秘密
摇曳的雪花却迷离了我的眼底
我去雄奇的泰山，寻你
那里见证过我俩攀登的足迹
飞扬的雪花却将上山的路封闭
我去北国的城市，寻你
那里曾留下我俩做义工的汗滴
漫天的雪花却把我淹没在小巷里
我去美丽的海边，寻你
那里有我俩蜜月的甜蜜
茫茫的雪花却将往事飘落在大海里
我去辽阔的锡林郭勒草原，寻你
那里曾是我俩创业的土地
破旧的厂房却被大雪尘封在记忆里
亲爱的人啊
你一定是变成了雪花
融化在了我的梦里

2018.1.8

Looking for You

Where are you?
I went to the grove near the village to look for you,
Where we played together when we were young
But the thick snow covered our childhood interest.
I went to our alma mater to look for you,
In which the secret record of our dating life was kept.
But the falling snowflakes blurred my eyes.
I went to the magnificent Mountain Tai to look for you,
Which witnessed our climbing footsteps
But the falling snowflakes closed the mountain road.
I went to the city in the north to look for you,
Where we worked as volunteers
But the endless amount of snow submerged me in the alley.
I went to the beautiful seaside to look for you,
Where we had our sweet honeymoon
But the vast amount of snowflakes made the past fall into the sea.
I went to the vast Xilin Gol Grassland to look for you,
Where we started up our business
But the dilapidated factory was covered by the heavy snow.
My lover
You must have turned into a snowflake,
Thawing in my dream.

January 8, 2018

红牡丹和睡莲

你健壮躯体下
一朵红牡丹，娇艳
轻吻，摘下娇羞潋滟
两片花瓣丰满，包不住你伟岸的桥
灵魂，无法抵达彼岸
温柔的野蛮，窒息了短暂的春天
孤独撞击夜晚，呻吟洒落
一片亮晶晶，不敢睁眼
怕你狰狞的脸，撕碎了从前
也许，我只能做你梦里的睡莲

2018.1.2

Red Peony and Water Lily

Underneath your strong body,

I'm a beautiful red peony.

You kiss me tenderly,

Taking off my shyness.

Two plump petals can't hold your strong cowry.

My soul is unable to reach your heart.

Using your gentle brutality,

You suffocate my short spring.

My loneliness hits the night,

Moaning and scattering everywhere.

I dare not open my eyes

Because I'm afraid your hideous face will tear our past to shreds.

Maybe I can only be as water lily in your dream.

January 2, 2018

地平线

路太远
我不会把你阻拦
望着你的背影
我默默无言
梦里湿漉漉的思念
早已埋进远远的地平线

2017.12.30

Horizon

The journey is too far

And I will not stop you.

Watching you from behind,

I remain silent

Because my deep longing for you in my dream

Has been buried into the distant horizon.

December 30, 2017

雪 花

我是一片，摇曳的雪花
从遥远的天堂，寻你而来
夏天早已不见，秋天也已走远
望着你的背影，我只有紧追慢赶
亲爱的人啊，就让我轻轻飘落在你双肩
纵然你把我抖落，我也心甘情愿
起码我曾见过，你美丽的容颜
即使追不上你，也要飘落在你身后
化作春水，滋润相思的冬天

2017.12.14

Snowflake

I am a dancing snowflake,

Coming from a faraway paradise to look for you.

Because summer has already gone

And autumn is also far away,

I only look at your back, running hard after you.

My lover, allow me to fall gently on your shoulders.

I'm still willing to do it if you shake me off

Because at least I've seen your beautiful face.

Even if I can't catch up with you, I will fall behind you,

Becoming spring water to moisten the lovesick winter.

December 14, 2017

爱情来了无法阻挡

走过红尘沧桑

以为自己理性而顽强

遇见你，我却乖乖向你投降

平静的内心掀起波涛万丈

亲爱的人啊，在你面前

我不想再假装冷酷刚强

我愿变成一只小船

在你温柔的港湾里轻轻摇荡

爱情总是防不胜防

爱情来了无法阻挡

2017.12.2

Love Cannot Be Refused

Having experienced many aspects of love,
I think I'm rational and tenacious.
I surrender to you obediently when I meet you because
You make me excited like the waves against the sky in my heart.
My love, in front of you
I don't want to pretend to be cool and strong.
I would like to become a boat,
Swaying lightly in your gentle harbor.
Love is always hard to detect
And you can't refuse her when she comes.

December 2, 2017

如　果

如果，落叶飘零
是离别的忧伤
我愿做最后一抹夕阳
为干瘪的爱情涂上一层金黄

如果，孤独
是爱情的奖赏
我愿做荒芜草原上的孤狼
奔向梦里爱情的天堂

如果，爱情
停止了生长
我愿化作泥土
孕育来春生命的希望

2017.11.22

If

If falling leaves
Are the sadness of departure,
I would like to be the last ray of sunshine,
Applying shriveled love with gold.

If loneliness
Is the reward of love,
I would like to be a lone wolf on the wild grassland,
Running to the paradise of love in my dream.

If love
Stops growing,
I would like to turn into soil,
To give birth to the hope of spring.

November 22, 2017

爱之歌

你是春天的花朵

我就是你身边的绿叶，衬托出你的娇媚

你是夏夜的花香

我就是微风，跟随你河边徜徉

你是秋天红彤彤的苹果

我就是树下的果农，把你轻轻摘下放在心窝

你是冬天的太阳

我就是高高的雪山，映出你绚丽的光泽

你是一团燃不尽的大火

我就是沉默的冰，融化在你心窝

你是一首美妙的交响乐

我就是一个跳动的音符，与你精诚合作

你是一幅美丽的图画

我就是画中的小鸟，为你唱起生命的歌

你是一支浪漫的舞曲

我就是你脚下的舞鞋，托起你轻盈的梦

你是开闸的洪水

我就是汹涌的波浪，随你漂泊

你是辽阔的草原

我就是奔腾的野马，脚步永不停歇

你是温暖肥美的沃土

我就是勤恳的农夫，耕耘出爱情的硕果

2017.11.21

Song of Love

You are a flower in spring and

I am the green leaves around you to make you more charming.

You are the fragrance of a summer flower in the evening and

I am the breeze, following you to wander by the river.

You are a red apple and

I am the fruit farmer under the tree who gently picks you and puts you
    in my heart.

You are the sun in winter and

I am the high snow-capped mountains, reflecting your brilliant luster.

You are an endless fire and

I am a block of silent ice, melting in your heart.

You are a wonderful symphony and

I am a beating note, cooperating with you sincerely.

You are a beautiful picture and

I am the bird in your painting, singing a song of life for you.

You are a romantic dance music and

I am your dance shoes under your feet, supporting your light dream.

You are the flood that opens the the gate and

I am the surging waves, drifting with you.

You are a vast grassland and

I am a wild galloping horse, never stopping to rest.

You are the warm fertile soil, and

I am a diligent farmer, cultivating the fruits of love.

November 21, 2017

一朵花的距离

我与你，一朵花的距离
你不说，我不语
淡淡的花香，迷醉了自己
睁开眼睛，分不清是花还是你
别靠近，别远离
朦胧的美丽，丝丝的甜蜜
梦里醒来，嘴角是一抹青春的笑意

2016.4.11

A Flower Between You and Me

A flower is between you and me

Which keeps us quiet.

The light fragrance enchants me so much

That I can't tell you from the flower

When I open my eyes.

Please neither close to me nor keep away from me

To make me feel the hazy beauty and the slightest sweetness.

When I wake up, there is a little youthful smile on my face.

April 11, 2016

习　惯

习惯了角落里伤痛
习惯了深夜里清醒
习惯了人群中安静
习惯了没你的日子
独自旅行

2016.8.15

Being Used To

I'm used to suffering in the corner.

I'm used to waking up at midnight.

I'm used to being quiet in the crowd.

I'm used to traveling alone

Without you.

August 15, 2016

你、我

如果，你是春天
我就是一朵花儿
在你温暖的怀抱里
绽放青春浪漫

如果，你是夏天
我就是一棵翠竹
在你激情的世界里
节节向上

如果，你是秋天
我就是一棵红高粱
在你博大和谐的土地上
成熟而饱满

如果，你是冬天
我就是一片飞舞的雪花
在你深沉内敛的天空里
为你增添一份生命的内涵

2017.10.13

You, I

If you were spring,
I'd be a flower,
Blooming my youthful romance
In your warm embrace.

If you were summer,
I'd be a shoot,
Growing taller and taller
In your passionate world.

If you were fall,
I'd be a red sorghum,
Becoming mature and full
In your vast land.

If you were winter,
I'd be a flying snowflake,
Adding meaning to your life
In your vast and unrestrained sky.

October 13, 2017

花

我是一朵，飞在天上的花
俯视着茫茫大地，寻找着属于自己的家
希望我能看到你，你也能看到我
祈求上苍，别让我俩错过
亲爱的人啊，请张开双臂迎接我
让我在你的枝头轻轻落下，绽放青春芳华
如果找不到你，我只有在秋风里飘落
落在草原田野，落在山峦湖泊
等你，等你来找我
如果你找不到我，我就化作泥土
等你，等你来踩我
我好亲吻你，美丽的脚丫
编织成梦里，最美的童话

2017.10.5

Flower

I am a flower, flying in the sky,

Overlooking the vast land to look for my own home.

I hope I can see you and you can see me, too.

I pray to heaven that we would not miss each other.

My darling, please open your arms to meet me and

Let me fall lightly on your branches, blooming in the springtime.

If I can not find you, I will have to fall in the autumn wind,

Falling on the grasslands, fields, mountains and lakes,

Waiting, waiting for you to come to me.

If you can not find me, I will turn into the soil,

Waiting, waiting for you to step on me

So that I can kiss your beautiful feet

To weave a beautiful fairy tale in my dream.

October 5, 2017

我　怕

从没告诉过你，我怕
怕你的爱像春雨
只把我湿润一点点
怕你的爱像夏天的烈日
让我无处躲闪
怕你的爱像秋雨
给我无尽的纠缠
怕你的爱像冬日的地窖
让我看不见阳光灿烂
我只有躲在梦里
悄悄抚平心中的波澜
在你面前风轻云淡
默默看着你渐行渐远
今晚，月光洒落湖面
微风，掠过我的琴弦
不经意想起，海那边的你
曾映入我的眼

2017.9.28

I'm Afraid

I have never told you I'm afraid.

I'm afraid your love is like the spring rain

Which makes me a little wet.

I'm afraid your love is like the hot summer sun

Which makes me have no place to hide.

I'm afraid your love is like the autumn rain

Which entangles me endlessly.

I'm afraid your love is like the winter cellar

Which keeps me away from the bright sunshine.

I can only hide in my dream,

Repressing my infinite love to you.

I keep calm in front of you,

Silently watching you drift away.

Tonight, the moonlight is shining over the lake

And the night breeze is playing my strings.

Inadvertently, I think of you

Who are living on the other side of the sea

And have been on my mind.

September 28, 2017

丢

你可以丢了我
只要你快乐
我也可以丢了你
我却无法像你一样洒脱
我想把你丢在春天里
你却变成美丽的花朵诱惑我
我想把你丢在夏天里
你却化作大雨滂沱淋透了我
我想把你丢在秋天里
你却化作绵绵细雨缠绕着我
我想把你丢在冬天里
你却变成纷飞的雪花迷乱了我

2017.9.25

Forgetting

You can forget me

As long as you are happy.

I can also forget you

But I can't be as free and at ease as you.

I want to forget you in spring

But you become the beautiful flowers and seduce me.

I want to forget you in summer

But you turn into a rainstorm and drench me.

I want to forget you in the fall

But you become a continuous rain and twine me.

I want to forget you in winter

But you become the flying snowflakes and confuse me.

September 25, 2017

一个遥远的地方

多想，和你一起去
一个遥远的地方
那里，有一座小木房
坐落在小山旁
白云在蓝天上游荡
山谷间翠鸟歌唱
风儿送来阵阵花香
我用多情的眼睛
把四季里的你珍藏
我用朝阳为你洗脸
洗去你昨夜脸上淡淡的忧伤
我摘下绿叶为你做衣裳
衬托出你花儿一样的脸庞
我用火热的心房
深夜里温暖你冰冷的过往
让时光在彼此的皱纹里慢慢流淌
流进房前的小河里
静静流向远方

2017.9.24

A Faraway Place

I long to go

To to a faraway place with you

Where there is a small wooden house

Which lies at the foot of a hill.

The white clouds are floating in the blue sky,

The kingfisher is singing in the valley

And the refreshing breeze is sending us the flower fragrance.

I use my amorous eyes

To treasure you in the four seasons.

I wash your face with the sunshine in the morning

To wash away the tiny sadness on your face from last night.

I pick the green leaves to make a dress for you

To bring out your face like a flower.

I use my fiery-hot heart

To warm your cold past late at night.

Let time flow slowly in our wrinkles,

Flowing into the brook in front of the house

And flowing away quietly.

September 24, 2017

我裸露的爱

一路春风追你
十里桃花闻香
我裸露的爱
不穿衣裳
你在哪里绽放
我就在哪里徜徉
拈花惹草不思量
看你如何再躲藏

2017. 8. 23

My Naked Love

Chasing you in the spring breeze,

I smell your pleasant fragrance all the way.

My naked love

Never wears clothes.

Wherever you are blooming,

I will wander there.

I love you without hesitation.

How can you hide again?

August 23, 2017

改　变

不自觉，开始打扮
节食减肥，身材更加曲线
省吃俭用，买一件时尚有品位的衣衫
精细化妆，把美丽完美呈现
温柔性情，绽放女人的春天
一切改变，只为惊艳你清澈的眼
碰上你，我躲在人群后边
发呆，偷笑，又怕被人发现
想对你说的话，心里重复了无数遍
爱情火焰，已被你点燃
缘分，没有长眼
爱情，需要勇敢
最美的时刻，怎能拖延
心仪的人啊，我要走向你
即使飞蛾扑火，也要与你爱恋

2017.8.14

Changing

Unconsciously, I begin to dress up

And go on a diet to have a curvier figure.

I live frugally to buy a fashionable and tasteful dress,

Putting on make-up carefully to show a perfect appearance.

A gentle temperament makes a woman's spring bloom.

All changes are just to surprise your clear eyes.

I hide behind the crowd when I meet you,

Lost in thought, laughing and afraid of being found.

My heart has repeated what I want to say many times

Because the flame of love has been ignited by you.

Destiny has no eyes

And love needs the courage.

This is the most beautiful moment, how can you delay?

My love, I will walk to you!

I'll love you even though our love has no final ending.

August 14, 2017

花枝招展

那天，你穿了一件
我喜欢的白衬衫
灿烂的阳光，把忧伤晒干
缘分的藤条，从此交缠
我说你浪，你说我漫
今生我俩，一起浪漫
为了生命无憾，爱情圆满
每天深夜，我愿踏着月光
探寻幽深的伊甸园
采集带着露珠的花朵
把思念的花篮装满
悄悄挂在你窗前
等你早上，掀开窗帘
阳光，洒满花朵
还有你俊俏的脸
迟到的春天
依然会花枝招展

2017.8.11

Blooming Gorgeously

That day you were wearing a white shirt

Which the one I like the most.

My depression was dried up in the bright sunshine,

And the rattans of destiny began to intertwine from then on.

I say you are romantic and you say I am romantic

And we are both romantic together.

In order to live without regret and have perfect love,

I walk in the moonlight every night,

To seek the deep and quiet Eden,

Picking flowers with dewdrops,

And filling the basket of love with them.

I hang the basket of flowers in your window quietly,

Waiting for you to open the curtains in the morning,

Then the sunshine will kiss the flowers

And your pretty and charming face.

Late spring

Will still bloom gorgeously.

August 11, 2017

太阳雨

思念，堆积成山
站在山巅，遥望对岸
那里阳光灿烂，花海一片
分不清哪是你俊俏的脸
捧一把思念的泪水
轻轻撒进阳光里斑斓
太阳雨打湿了你美丽的裙边
你不经意抬起头
一道彩虹挂在你凝望的蓝天
那是我开心的笑脸
默默告诉你
我从未走远

2017.8.3

Sun Shower

My love is like a mountain

And I'm standing on the mountaintop, looking down to the other side

Where the sun is shining and there is a sea of flowers

But I can't tell where you are.

I hold the tears of yearning in my hands

And throw them gently into the sunshine.

The rain shower makes your beautiful skirt wet,

So you carelessly raise your head,

Finding a rainbow hanging in the blue sky.

It is my smiling face

Which quietly tells you

I will never be far away.

August 3, 2017

等 待

用最后一点年轻
摇曳梦中的风景
站在记忆的海边
等待那阵阵海风
等待你脚步匆匆
等待大海上最后一抹鲜红
迟到的爱情值得等

2017.8.1

Waiting

Cherishing the last days of my youth,

I'm swaying in the scenery in my dream.

Standing on the seaside of memory lane,

I'm waiting for the sea breeze,

Waiting for your hurrying footsteps

And waiting for the last ray of sunlight glowing over the sea.

The late love is worth the wait.

August 1, 2017

夏 天

一身布衣
一杯茶盏
斜倚在藤椅中
沐浴夏日清风潋滟
露台上翠绿的藤蔓
把腰肢尽情舒展
丝竹声淡淡
将思绪浸满
远方的你
何时来到我身边
欣赏雨后晚霞满天
一起把余生过完

2017.7.19

Summer

Wearing a cttton gown

And holding a cup of tea,

I'm reclining in the rattan chair,

Showering the cool summer breeze rippling.

The emerald vines on the terrace

Unfold its branches freely.

The music is lightly playing,

Filling my thoughts.

You are far away.

When will you come to me?

Let's enjoy the sunset after the rain,

Spending the rest of our lives together.

July 19, 2017

懂

云懂山的孤单
山懂云的缠绵
叶懂花的期盼
花懂叶的无言
我懂你沉默不语
你懂我欲言又止
你懂我的脆弱
我懂你的坚强
你不必说谎
我也不必逞强
因为相爱的人
会懂彼此所有的模样

2017.7.14

Understanding

The cloud knows the loneliness of the mountain

And the mountain knows the lingering of the cloud.

The leaf understands the hope of the flower

And the flower knows the silence of the leaf.

I understand your silence

And you know my unspoken words.

You understand my fragility

And I know your adamancy.

You do not have to lie

And I need not flaunt my superiority

Because people who fall in love

Understand all the behaviors of each other.

July 14, 2017

如果你爱我，请别对我说

如果你爱我，请别对我说
我会变成一缕春风
轻轻抚摸你峥嵘的岁月
温柔你一生爱的执着

如果你爱我，请别对我说
我会变成一朵莲花
悄悄绽放在你的梦里
倾听你爱情的诉说

如果你爱我，请别对我说
我会变成一夜秋雨
静静氤氲在你的世界
陪着你无边的伤感和寂寞

如果你爱我，请别对我说
我会变成一片雪花
偷偷飘落在你的心窝
滋润你干涸的心河

2017.6.30

If You Love Me, Please Do Not Tell Me

If you love me, please do not tell me
Because I will turn into spring breeze,
Stroking your extraordinary life softly
And tenderly clinging to the love of your life.

If you love me, please do not tell me
Because I will become a lotus,
Blooming quietly in your dream,
And listening carefully to your tales of love.

If you love me, please do not tell me
Because I will turn into a night of autumn rain,
Silently filling your world
And accompanying your inexplicable sadness and loneliness.

If you love me, please do not tell me
Because I will become a snowflake,
Secretly falling into your heart
And moistening the dry river in your heart.

June 30, 2017

如果那样，我不会出来

听说，你要来
我种下许多花，一路盛开
躲在花丛后
我静静等待你的到来
请你不要早到
那时花儿还没有色彩
你也不要迟到
否则花儿会开败
如果你只是偶尔路过
折一束桃花枝游玩
过后一扔，不再理睬
如果那样，我不会出来
青春的花枝上
不该挂满忧伤和无奈
我宁愿默默看着你
簇拥着花枝离开
我轻轻告诉春天
明年春暖，花儿还会再开

2017.6.18

If That's the Case, I Will Not Come Out

I heard that you are coming so I planted

Many blooming flowers along the path you would travel.

I'm hiding behind the flowers,

Quietly waiting for your arrival.

Please don't come early

Because the flowers have no color.

Please don't be late otherwise

The flowers will be withered.

If you only occasionally pass by

And break off a peach branch to play

Then throw it away and forget it,

I will not come out

Because sadness and helplessness

Shouldn't hang on the youthful branch.

I would rather quietly watch your leaving in silence

With an an armful of flowers.

I gently tell spring

The flowers will bloom again next spring.

June 18, 2017

你是我四季的花

如果你是春天里的一朵梨花
我就是围绕在你身边的一只蝴蝶
用生命为你舞出爱情的执着
永不疲倦和寂寞

如果你是夏日里的一朵荷花
我就是站立在你肩膀上的一只蜻蜓
轻轻向你把相思诉说
一起拥抱爱情的高洁

如果你是秋日里一朵菊花
我就是你脚下肥沃的土地
为你绽放提供养料和依靠
秋风里默默祈祷爱情不要飘落

如果你是冬日里的一片雪花
我就是早上那缕温暖的阳光
把你融化在我的心里
黑夜里拥抱着你

2017.6.16

You Are My Flowers of the Four Seasons

If you were a pear flower in spring,
I'd like to be a butterfly flying around you,
Dancing for our love with my life
And never being tired and lonely.

If you were a lotus flower in summer,
I'd like to be a dragonfly standing on your shoulders,
Telling my love to you gently
And embracing the beautiful love together.

If you were a chrysanthemum in autumn,
I'd like to be the fertile land where you grow,
Providing you with the nutrients and sustenance,
And praying that the love will continue.

If you were a snowflake in winter,
I'd like to be the warm sunshine in the morning,
Melting you into my heart
And embracing you at night.

June 16, 2017

宁缺毋滥

相距并不遥远
你我却不曾相见
知道梦里的你我
没有多少改变
对望中默默无言
时空里淡淡思念
没有你的日子
我宁缺毋滥
等花开花落
天堂里与你再续前缘

2017.6.1

The Best Is Worth Waiting

The distance between us is not far

But we haven't ever met.

I know in our dreams

There isn't much change.

Staring at each other quietly,

We miss with a faint longing.

It's better to have nothing if I can have you.

Because you are worth waiting for.

We will love again in heaven

Where the flowers bloom and fall.

June 1, 2017

寻

春天收藏起花香
冬天遮挡住太阳
浪人离开了孤街
野猫逃离了小巷
黑夜躲避着月亮
相思溜出了心房
寻不到梦里姑娘

2017.5.28

Looking For

The fragrance of flowers is collected in spring.

The sun is sheltered in winter.

The wanderers left the lonely street

And the wildcat fled the alley.

The night eludes the moon

And my lovesickness slips out of my heart

But I can not find the girl in my dream.

May 28, 2017

观　望

自行车前后轮的爱情
注定没有结果
但他俩却爱得执着
车身支架将他俩连接起
却也将两人阻隔
一个在前一个在后
只有彼此关注默默诉说
既然属于同一辆自行车
就该肩负责任一起向前奔波
后轮吻遍前轮滚过的每一寸角落
回眸的前轮泪水婆娑
人生路上有你陪我
观望也是一种幸福的执着

2017.5.15

Watching and Waiting

Because of fate, the love of the front and rear wheels
Of a bicycle are doomed to have no result
But they love each other strongly.
The body frame connects both of them
But also divides both of them.
One is in the front and the other in the back and
They only have to pay attention to each other in silence.
Since we belong to the same bike,
We should be responsible to go forward together.
The rear wheel kisses every inch of the front wheel's track
And the front wheel glances back, crying.
Because you accompany me on the road of life,
Watching and waiting is also a happy persistence.

May 15, 2017

我愿做爱情的傻瓜

我愿做爱情的傻瓜
不去伤害别人
也不希望别人来伤害我
因为爱情本是温柔善良的执着

我愿做爱情的傻瓜
请不要告诉我你厌倦了我
只要悄悄离开我
我宁愿在相思里寻找寄托

我愿做爱情的傻瓜
相思在午夜的路灯下摇曳
我站在阳台上拥抱寂寞
告诉星空我曾爱过

我愿做爱情的傻瓜
不想在坚硬的城市里继续漂泊
只想有个温暖的家
每天有人陪着唠嗑

2017.5.14

I Would Like to Be a Fool of Love

I would like to be a fool of love.

I will not hurt other people.

I do not want others to hurt me, either.

Because love is the persistence of gentleness and kindness.

I would like to be a fool of love.

Please do not tell me you're tired of me.

Even though you leave me quietly,

I can have an expectation in lovesickness.

I would like to be a fool of love.

I miss you and wander under the streetlamp at midnight.

I stand on the balcony to embrace my loneliness,

Telling the starry sky that I have loved you.

I would like to be a fool of love.

I do not want to continue to wander in the hard city

And just want to have a warm home,

Chatting with my lover who accompanies me every day.

May 14, 2017

匆匆的春天

来不及欣赏你美丽的容颜
也来不及和你说一声再见
匆匆的你，不经意间已走远
留下一丝丝余香，飘进梦里边
也许，你嫁给了夏天
脱掉了美丽的花衬衫
躲进葱茏的绿色里，让我寻不见
也许，你嫁给了秋天
绵绵秋雨诉说着你的哀怨
伞下的我，独自徘徊在雨里边
也许，你嫁给了冬天
漫天的雪花覆盖了从前
留给寂寞的长夜，白茫茫一片

2017.4.28

Hasty Spring

It's too late to appreciate your beautiful face and
Too late to say goodbye to you,
I find you have left in a hurry and have gone far away,
Leaving a trace of fragrance floating in my dream.
Maybe you married summer
And took off your beautiful flower shirt and
Hid in the lush green, so I can not find you.
Maybe you married fall
Of which the endless rain tells me of your sorrow and
I wander in the rain with an umbrella.
Maybe you married winter
Of which the snowflakes cover the past,
Leaving a vast expanse of white.

April 28, 2017

有 你

有你，我就不怕了
漆黑的路上
你会来接我

有你，我就任性了
无理取闹后
你会哄我

有你，我就不羡慕别人了
两人的世界里
你一直履行着你爱的诺言

2017.4.13

Having You

Having you, I am not scared
Because you will come to pick me up
On the dark road.

Having you, I become wayward
Because after I make trouble without any reason,
You will coax me.

Having you, I do not envy others
Because in our world,
You have continuously fulfilled your promise of love.

April 13, 2017

老 城

护城河旁，阳光暖洋洋
弯弯的柳树，抚摸着斑驳的老城墙
温柔了沧桑的时光
城墙下孩子们玩耍的笑声
笑弯了护城河管理员笔挺的脊梁
城门口那棵高高的树上，玉兰静静开放
四溢的清香，沿着长长的小巷流淌
跟着小黄狗，来到小巷尽头的四合院
一枝绿萝，爬满青砖瓦墙
走进儿时欢乐的小院
鹅卵石小径旁的竹子，把我轻轻阻挡
掀开珠帘，拂去床头箱子上的尘埃
箱底你的几十封信，已经发黄
如果早知道，国外的月亮不比家乡的亮
你娟秀的字里，不会写满忧伤
擦干净供桌，把三庙香点燃
袅袅弥漫出你俊俏的脸庞
如果，生命可以逆生长
我不会离开，你我青梅竹马的地方
如果你愿意，下辈子
老城里，与你地老天荒

2017.3.28

Old Town

It is warm in the sunshine by the moat.

The soft willow branches are touching the mottled wall of the old
town,

Making the vicissitudes of time gentle.

Children are playing beside the wall and in the children's laughter,

The moat manager's waist is bent with age.

The tall magnolia flowers are blooming quietly near the gate

And their overflowing fragrance is flowing down the long alley.

Following a lovely yellow dog, I come to the courtyard at the end of the alley,

Whose wall is covered with scindapsus aureus.

Walking into the happy courtyard of childhood,

I am gently blocked by the bamboo.

I push aside the beaded curtain and wipe off the dust on the box at the
head of the bed.

Dozens of your letters in the bottom of the box have become yellow.

If I had known earlier that the foreign moon wasn't brighter than our
hometown's,

Your beautiful handwriting wouldn't have expressed your sadness.

Wipe the altar clean and light three temple incense sticks.

The diffusing smoke forms your beautiful face.

If life could grow in reverse,

I wouldn't have left the place where my childhood sweetheart lived.

If you like, in the next life,

I'll never leave you until the end of time.

March 28, 2017

总　想

总想，故乡的山冈
放学后你我一起背着书包
看梨花开放

总想，大学里的那片小树林
你依偎在我怀里
轻轻歌唱

总想，那个离别的夜晚
你飞往美国的航班
飞过我头顶上方

总想，那个不现实的理由
说服自己的彷徨
让你再回到我身旁

2017.3.20

I Always Think Of

I always think of the hills of our hometown.
After school, we carried our school bags
And watched the pear blooming together.

I always think of the grove in our university.
You snuggled up in my arms,
Singing gently.

I always think of the night you left.
Your plane to the United States
Flew over my head.

I always think of an unrealistic reason
To convince my indecision
To ask you to come back to me.

March 20, 2017

等待你卸下我的伪装

夜色,深沉
我关上蜗居的门
脱去职业装
温柔的水流
冲洗掉疲惫的灰尘
任意抚摸着寂寞的青春
你不是月光
黑夜里如何抚慰我的忧伤
你不是大树
烈日下如何给我阴凉
你不是海洋
我浪漫小船如何任意漂荡
兵荒马乱的坚硬都市里
我只有学会刀枪不入
男人般刚强
亲爱的人啊
我正站在岁月的车站
等待春天的列车
等待与你的邂逅
等待你卸下我的伪装
等待你赞美、呵护和欣赏
小鸟依人在你身旁
温柔的花儿只会因你而绽放

2017.3.18

Waiting for You to Remove My Camouflage

Late at night,

I close the door of my home.

Having taken off my business attire,

Soft water flows

Rinsing off the dust,

Touching freely my lonely young body.

You are not the moonlight,

How can you soothe my sorrow at night?

You are not a big tree,

How can you shade me from the hot sun?

You are not the ocean,

How can you make my romantic boat float freely?

In the chaos of the hard city,

I only learn to be invulnerable

And as strong as a man.

My dear,

I'm standing at the time station,

Waiting for the spring train,

Waiting to encounter you,

Waiting for you to remove my camouflage,

Waiting for your praise, care and appreciation.

I'll rest upon you like a little bird.

Tender flowers will bloom only because of you.

March 18, 2017

缘　分

我以为有一天
在青梅竹马的游戏里
在教学楼的过道上
在车间的机器轰鸣声中
在发黄的日记里
我会遇到你
然后发生一见钟情的奇迹
可你却没有出现
你到底在哪里
是在错过的机遇中
还是在门外的踟蹰里
我也曾在拥挤的人群中
搜索你明亮的眼睛
在深夜空寂的街道上
仔细聆听你偶尔路过的脚步声
在茫茫的雪原上
追寻你模糊的足迹
可我还是寻不到你
我问天，天不语
我问风，风吹干了我的泪滴
我躲在角落里
默默感受内心的孤寂
知道你，一定躲在某个地方
可你为何对我不搭理

2017.3.6

Destiny

I thought that one day
I would meet you
In the games of our childhood,
In the hallway of the teaching building,
In the rumbling sound of the machine in the workshop
And in the yellow diary.
I will meet you and fall in love at first sight.
But you haven't appeared yet.
Where on earth are you?
Are you in the missed opportunity
Or the hesitation outside the door?
I have also been in the crowd,
Searching for your bright eyes.
I have been in the quiet streets at night,
Listening carefully for your occasional footsteps to pass by.
I have been in the vast snowfield,
Pursuing your vague footprints.
But I still have not found you.
I ask the day and it keeps quiet.
I ask the wind and it dries my tears.
I hide in the corner.
I feel lonely inside.
I know that you must be hiding in a place,
But why do you not care for me?

March 6, 2017

春色关不住

把春天
深深锁在心间
围起冷漠的栅栏
怕春天的花枝
恣意蔓延
阻挡住我模糊的视线
寂寞的泪水
却悄悄溢出心田
默默浇灌着小院墙根下
那棵孤独的迎春花
绽开一树春天
告诉世界
爱情并没走远

2017.3.5

Spring Sneaking Out of My Mind

Lock spring

Deeply in the heart

And surround her by a cold fence.

I'm afraid of the spring flowers

Will Blossom waywardly

Which will block my blurred line of sight.

But the lonely tears

Quietly overflow in my heart and

Silently watering the lonely winter jasmine

Under the wall.

The jasmine blooms in spring

To tell the world

Love is not far away.

March 5, 2017

三　月

三月
是准备出嫁的春姑娘
柔风、细雨、小溪叮咚响
飘摇风筝，美丽衣裳
是她要带的嫁妆

三月
如新生的婴儿
小草，嫩绿尖尖
燕子呢喃，杨柳间
盈盈笑意，花枝招展

三月的故乡
在遥远的南方
那里没有寒冷和冰霜
只有莺飞草长
鸟语花香

我是三月的新郎
养一只布谷鸟
为她歌唱
种一树桃花
迎娶新娘，百里胭脂香

2017.3.2

March

March
Is the spring girl preparing to get married.
The soft wind, a fine rain, the sound of the creek,
A flying kite and a beautiful dress
Is the dowry she will bring.

March
Is like a newborn baby.
The grass is tender, thin and long.
The swallow is chirping, in the branches of the willow.
She's full of smiles and dresses gorgeously.

The hometown of March
Is in the far south.
There is no cold or frost
But orioles are flying, the grass is growing,
Birds are twittering and the flowers smell sweet.

I am the groom in March,
Raising a cuckoo
To sing to her.
In order to marry my bride, I'll plant many peaches
And their rouge incense will reach 100 miles away.

March 2, 2017

第三辑　风恶轻薄

醉

春天醉了，桃红柳绿，草长莺飞

夏天醉了，阳光灿烂，海天相随

秋天醉了，天高云淡，望穿秋水

冬天醉了，雪花翻飞，蜡梅吐蕊

漂泊在外的游子醉了，因为他想忘记寒冷和疲惫

放荡不羁的浪子醉了，因为他开始为曾经的鲁莽后悔

我也醉了，因为我又想起了你的美

遥远的你啊，请你举起酒杯，为我俩的曾经干杯

敬你第一杯，感谢你让我体会到了初恋的滋味

敬你第二杯，感谢你用温柔抹去了我沧桑的眼泪

敬你第三杯，感谢你默默付出却总说无怨无悔

如果时光可以倒流，我愿舍弃一切陪你走遍东西南北

如果生命可以轮回，我愿和你再次相依相偎

如果误解可以云开雾散，你也不会和我一刀两断远走高飞

如果执着能让我把你从国外追回，你也不会出意外让我痛彻心扉

今晚就让我彻底醉一回，然后去天堂和你相会，永远相陪

2018.12.25

Being Drunk

Spring is drunk, with the pink peaches, green willows, sprouting grass and flying orioles.

Summer is drunk, with the shining sun and the meeting of the sea and sky.

Autumn is drunk, with the vast sky and light clouds, gazing at the autumn water.

Winter is drunk, with the dancing snowflakes and the blossoming wintersweet.

The wanderer is drunk because he wants to forget the cold and fatigue.

The dissolute prodigal is drunk because he begins to regret his past reckless behavior.

I am also drunk because I am thinking of your beauty again.

We are far from each other, please raise a cup, drink a toast to our past.

My first toast to you is to thank you for allowing me to taste the first love.

My second toast to you is to thank you for wiping away my tears of vicissitudes with your tenderness.

My third toast to you is to thank you for always giving quietly without regrets.

If I could turn back time, I'd give up everything to accompany you around the world.

If life could be reincarnated, I would like to be with you again.

If misunderstandings had been cleared up, you would not have gone far away from me.

If my persistence could let me get you back from abroad, you would not have had the accident that broke my heart.

Let me get completely drunk tonight. Then go to heaven to meet you and be with you forever.

December 25, 2018

归还你的心

千方百计偷来你的心
我却无处安放
把它藏在春天里
它却红杏出墙
风流在十里春风里
把它藏在夏日里
它又化作彩虹
炫耀在雨后的天空上
把它藏在秋天里
它却化作秋雨
抚摸着每一个没伞的路人
把它藏在冬日里
它又化作一片雪花
不知落在了谁的窗前
我该如何对待你
还是把心还给你吧
那样我就心安了
从此不再迷恋
也不再痛苦难眠
只希望一觉醒来
回到相识的那一天
是你天真纯洁的笑脸
我俩的爱情重新上演

2018.11.26

Return Your Heart

I stole your heart by all means.

But I had nowhere to put it.

I hid it in spring

However, it had an affair secretly,

Reveling in the spring breeze.

I hid it in summer

But it turned into a rainbow,

Showing off in the sky after the rain

I hid it in autumn

Nevertheless, it turned into the autumn rain,

Touching each man without an umbrella.

I hid it in winter

Yet it changed into a piece of snowflake

And I didn't know on whose window it fell.

How should I treat you?

I'll return your heart

So that I can be at ease.

From now on I will have no crush on you

And no more pain or sleepless nights.

After a sound sleep, I just want

To come back to the day we met,

Seeing your innocent pure smiling face.

Our love will begin again.

September 26, 2018

墙

时间和距离
是一堵高高的墙
我拼命翻过去
你却已是别人的新娘
从此我再没闻过女人香
以为我能把你渐渐遗忘
往事却像常青藤
在墙根下疯长
爬满了整堵墙
覆盖了青春时光
也覆盖了余生的幻想
朝阳中一朵牵牛花
在常青藤里独自开放

2018.11.19

Wall

Distance and time

Are a tall wall.

I desperately climbed over it,

But you had become the bride of the other man.

Since then, I haven't smelled another woman's fragrance.

I thought I could gradually forget you,

But the past is like ivy,

Growing at the foot of the wall.

It covers the whole wall

And my years of youth.

It also covers fantasy for the rest of my life.

A morning glory in the morning sun

Is blooming alone in the thick ivy.

November 19, 2018

你是我的花朵

你是我的花朵
如果绽放
请你对我说
短暂的春天
我不想错过

你是我的花朵
风雨袭来
我却无法庇护你
痛苦的我
只有看着你花瓣飘落

你是我的花朵
我捧起地上的花瓣
轻轻撒在记忆的长河
看着你渐渐飘走
留给我无尽的寂寞

2017.4.8

You Are My Flower

You are my flower.
If you bloom,
Please tell me
Because I do not want to miss
The short spring.

You are my flower.
When the wind and rain comes,
I cannot protect you.
I can do nothing
But watch your petals falling in pain.

You are my flower.
I carefully pick up the petals on the ground
And gently scatter them in the river of my memory,
Watching you drift away gradually.
You leave me in endless loneliness.

April 8, 2017

樱　花

知道梦里的你，来去匆匆
我屏住呼吸，生怕把你弄醒
你却自己偷偷溜出来
绽放如云霞，活泼似精灵
一阵风雨，却让你过早凋零
敲碎了我昨晚的梦
我捧起花瓣，告诉春天不疼
和你说过多少次，风雨不懂
我闭上眼，问春天
来年，能否和你再次相逢

2017.4.7

Sakura

I know you come and go hurriedly in my dream,

So I hold my breath in order not to wake you up,

But you sneak out,

Blooming like clouds and lively as a fairy.

A gust of wind and a shower of rain, however, make you die early,

Which shattered my dream last night.

I hold the petals in my hands, telling spring that it doesn't hurt.

I have told you many times that the wind and rain do not understand.

I close my eyes and ask spring

Whether I can meet you again next year.

April 7 , 2017

恋爱是一场雨

爱恋，是一场雨
淋湿了心，感冒了自己
回头，只有自己一个人
孤零零站在雨里

2016.8.8

Love Is Like a Rain

Love is like a rain

Which wets my heart and makes me catch a cold.

Turning around, I find myself,

Standing alone in the rain.

August 8, 2016

为你腾出空间

看着你寂寞的眼

我不想再假装

我俩的爱情美满

你沉默的心里

无奈装得太满

以为我俩会永远

可昨天太短

缘分太浅

轻轻收拾起

丢弃一地的爱恋

默默走出你的视线

为你腾出空间

2017.1.13

Make Room for You

Seeing the loneliness in your eyes,
I do not want to pretend
That our love is happy.
There is too much unwillingness
In your quiet heart.
I thought our love would last forever
But yesterday was too short
And luck is too shallow.
I gently picked up the pieces of our love
Which you discarded on the ground.
I silently walked out of your vision
To make room for you.

January 13, 2017

没有你,我什么都不是

总想忘记

你却鲜活在记忆里

被你爱过后

别人总走不进心底

你的好,每天在梦里

你知道我是大男子主义

知道我爱吃炸酥的黄花鱼

知道我喜欢用大衣把你藏在怀里

知道我有心事喜欢埋在心里

懵懂的青春,感谢有你

怀念我把脏衣服给你,让你洗

怀念你想尽办法逗我开心

我却发脾气

怀念你喂我吃药

可我躺在病床上爱理不理

怀念你躺在我怀里翻看我俩的照片

撒娇淘气

怀念躺在你腿上你帮我掏耳朵

温馨的你

怀念你从不称呼我爸我妈

一直都是咱爸咱妈

怀念你每天睡觉前微信里发的晚安

还有亲亲你

你总在付出,我却总是一次次伤害你

I'm Nothing Without You

I always want to forget you

But you're alive in my memory.

After being loved by you

I have no way to let others get into my heart.

Your love for me is in my dream every day.

You know I am a male chauvinist.

You know I like to eat the fried crispy yellow croaker.

You know I like to use my coat to hide you in my arms.

You know I like to keep things in my heart.

I'm grateful to have you in my life when I was young and ignorant.

I cherish the memory when you washed my dirty clothes,

Cherishing the memory of the scene in which you tried to make me
   happy when I lost my temper,

Cherishing the memory of the scene in which you gave me medicine
   while I standoffishly laid in hospital bed,

Cherishing the memory of the scene in which you were lying in my
   arms, looking at our photos and being naughty,

Cherishing the memory of the scene in which I was lying in your lap
   and you cleaned my ears,

Cherishing the memory of the scene in which you never addressed your
   parents as "mine" but always called them "our" father and "our"
   mother,

Cherishing the memory of the scene in which you said "good night"
   and "kiss you" on WeChat every night before going to bed.

You always gave everything to me, but I always hurt you.

我知道，你包容，你委屈
我知道，我混蛋，我自私
一次次争吵，一次次赌气
你终于累了，我终于失去了你
你说在你最爱我的时候，我不要你了
我说在我更爱你的时候，你也不要我了
那天你从身后抱住了我，号啕大哭
我还是毅然挣脱掉你，躲进宿舍默默哭泣
没人比你对我更好了，可我始终没有学会珍惜
后来有了新女朋友，我还是没法忘记你
等我学会了如何去爱，你却早已不在
世界太小，那天在纽约无意看见了你
和你手拉手的人已不是自己
眼泪中终于明白，没有你
我什么都没有，什么都不是
爱情一旦错过，再不会回来
你已消失在人海，我却站在岸边徘徊
亲爱的人啊，让我俩回到原点
让我再追你一次，还回你的爱

2018.9.4

I knew you were tolerant and wronged.

I knew I was an asshole and I was selfish.

We quarreled again and again and we were furious time and time again.

At last you were tired and I lost you.

You told me I abandoned you when you loved me most.

I told you you didn't want me when I began to love you more.

That day you hugged me from behind, crying loudly.

I still squirmed out of your arms resolutely and hid in the dormitory, crying silently.

You were the girl who loved me most in the world but I never learned how to cherish you.

Later I had a new girlfriend but I still could not forget you.

When I knew how to love, you have already gone.

The world is too small I inadvertently saw you in New York that day

But the person whom you held hands with was not me any more.

In my tears I finally understand

I'm nothing without you.

Love, like ours, once fled, never returns any more.

You disappeared in the sea of people, but I'm standing on the shore, lingering.

My dear lover, let's go back to the beginning.

Let me chase you again and return your love!

September 4, 2018

来生，我俩是否还能续缘

生命，一天天缩短
思念，一天天积攒
曾是一只燕子
自由飞过你美丽的春天
曾是一缕夏日的晚风
轻轻亲吻你俊俏的脸
曾是一枚落叶
悄悄飘落在你的面前
曾是一片雪花
温柔抚摸你性感的秀肩
以为我俩爱情会圆满
终究最后还是说再见
往事已成沧海桑田
也许爱得太晚
也许爱得太浅
彼此不再纠缠
隔岸相望，默默无言
不经意，已到暮年
你的容貌，变得遥远
来生，我俩是否还能续缘

2018.9.3

Love Each Other in the Afterlife

My life is getting shorter and shorter

But I miss you more and more.

Once I was a swallow,

Flying freely through your beautiful spring.

Once I was the breeze in the summer evening,

Softly kissing your pretty face.

Once I was a falling leaf,

Falling down quietly in front of your face.

Once I was a snowflake,

Gently touching your sexy shoulder.

I thought our love would be perfect

But in the end we said goodbye.

Our love has come and gone.

Maybe we loved each other too late

Or we didn't love each other enough.

We are no longer entangled with each other.

Facing each other from opposite shores, we remain silent.

Naturally, we are already old.

Your image is no longer clear in my mind.

Can we continue to love each other in the afterlife?

September 3, 2018

秋

低头
水中
你娇羞的温柔
抬头
你已走
满目是秋

2018.8.17

Autumn

When I looked down,
I saw your coy tenderness
In the water.
When I looked up,
You had already left.
It's always autumn in my eyes.

August 17, 2018

也许，我不好

也许，我不好
让你重新把爱情寻找
知道你身边有个他
他一定不像我
把事业看得比你重要
我也知道孤寂谁都受不了

也许，我不好
我不想告诉你
其实你和他的故事
我什么都知道
只是我不想让真相
成为你离开我的最后一根稻草

也许，我不好
谢谢你告诉我
他对你的好
虽然恨不得杀人
但我还是想忘记他
因为两人的故事里不该有仨

也许，我不好
请你千万别告诉我
你对他哪怕丁点儿的好

Perhaps, I'm No Good

Perhaps, I'm no good

Because you've begun to look for love again.

I know there is a man who is beside you.

He is certainly not like me

Putting career above you.

I also know nobody can stand loneliness.

Perhaps, I'm no good.

I don't want to tell you

In fact, I know

Everything about your story.

I just don't want the truth to be

The last straw for you to leave me.

Perhaps, I'm no good.

Thank you for telling me

He is good to you.

I'm so angry that I want to kill him

But I had better forget him

Because there shouldn't be three people in a love story.

Perhaps, I'm no good.

Please don't tell me

You love him, even a little bit,

起码这样我还能欺骗自己
以为我还是你心里唯一的宝
像以前一样相信你我的爱情天荒地老

也许，我不好
你泪流满面
让我心如刀绞
男人的尊严
在你面前这次我可以不要
只要你别再跟着他到处跑

也许，我不好
我无法忘记
你曾经对我的好
为了这个家
我还是选择原谅你
因为我说过爱你到老

2018.6.10

So I can cheat myself,

Believing I'm still the only treasure in your heart

And our love will last forever.

Perhaps, I'm no good.

The tears streaming down your cheek

Are breaking my heart.

I can lose my dignity as a man

In front of you this time

But you mustn't follow him everywhere.

Perhaps, I'm no good.

I can't forget you

Because you were good to me.

For the sake of the family,

I still choose to forgive you

Because I told you I would love you forever.

June 10, 2018

夜里的花

你从没见过我真正的样子
我是一朵只在夜里开的花
生在淤泥里，长在雾霾中
五颜六色的颗粒团团围绕着我
淡蓝色的忧伤，灰白色的痛苦，铜质色的欢乐
合成一汪黑色，浸染了我的肢体
黑色的花瓣依然绽放着执着
躲在黑暗的角落里
独自摇曳，如猫头鹰
窥视着白天狂欢后
世界的寂寞
尘世间的爱恨情仇
水一般从身旁流过
激情与冷漠，征服和反抗
施虐与受虐，伤口与快感
忧伤和欢乐，一切的一切
被无边的黑暗淹没
唯有梦里你的微笑
在眼前闪烁

2018.8.12

Night Flower

You've never seen me the way I really am.
I am a flower that only blooms at night.
I was born in the muck and grow in the haze.
Clumps of colorful particles surround me.
Pale blue sadness, grey pain and copper happiness
Blend into black which contaminates my body.
My black petals are still blooming persistently.
I'm hiding in a dark corner, swaying alone.
I'm like an owl
Who's peeping at the loneliness of the world
After the carnival in the daytime.
Love and hate of the world
Flow past me like water.
Passion and indifference, conquest and rebellion,
Sadism and masochism, wound and pleasure
Sorrow and joy, and everything
Are drowned by the immensity of darkness.
Only your smile in my dream
Is twinkling in front of me.

August 12, 2018

不　要

不要给我太多
不要给我任何承诺
不要发誓对我负责
不要深深记得我
只要能偶尔想起我
想起我曾为你失魂落魄
想起我俩多年的拍拖
想起为你我曾不食人间烟火
想起现在我不知道该说什么

2018.7.8

Do Not

Do not give me too much,

Do not promise me anything,

Do not vow to be responsible for me,

Do not remember me deeply,

Just think of me occasionally,

Think of the time when I lost my soul for you,

Think of the years we dated,

Think of my stay away from the crowd for you,

Think of the present when I don't know what to say.

July 8, 2018

一同死去

你我，明天
就要说再会
我俩，今晚
就用酒精麻醉
不想隐藏忧伤
更不想让你太累
看你日益憔悴
我的心已碎
迟到的春天里
玫瑰不该枯萎
红尘一世缘
今生为了谁
世俗的桎梏
锁不住思念的秋水
冷酷的世界
挡不住缘分的追随
你不该有丁点委屈
你不该深夜里流泪
亲爱的人啊
你看那小酒杯
多像一朵盛开的玫瑰
请再喝一杯
彻底醉一回
最好一起醉死

Die Together

Tomorrow we will

Say goodbye to each other.

Let's drink alcohol tonight

To anaesthetize ourselves.

I don't want to hide my sadness

And I don't want you to be too tired.

Seeing you become withered day by day,

My heart is broken.

In late spring,

A rose should not wither.

In the world of mortals,

For whom I live a life?

The shackles of the world

Can not lock the thoughts of autumn water.

The cold world

Can not stop our pursuit of love.

You should not suffer even a little grievance.

And you should not cry at night.

My dear baby,

Look at the little wine glass

Which is like a blooming rose.

Please have another drink

And get completely drunk.

I hope that Bacchus will drown us.

极乐世界里
你我永远相依相偎
再不会有人阻止
再不会让思念成灰
爱情的极致
就是一同死去
不留后悔

2018.7.4

So in heaven,

We will be together forever.

No one can separate us again.

I'll never let my thoughts turn to ashes again.

The pinnacle of love

Is to die together,

Leaving no regrets.

July 4, 2018

你走吧

你走吧
走得越远越好
不能千山万水
就还你一马平川
既然违背了诺言
就让爱情沧海桑田

你走吧
走得越远越好
距离是无法逾越的高山
爱情只有望洋兴叹
时间是大江东去
让爱情一去不复返

你走吧
走得越远越好
那样我才死心
不再执着
独自面对滚滚红尘
不再难过

你走吧
走得越远越好
有回忆陪着我

Get Away From Me

Get away from me,

The farther, the better.

You can't share my joys and sorrows,

So you are free to pursue a new love.

Since you have broken your promise,

Let's stop loving each other quickly.

Get away from me,

The farther, the better.

The distance is like a high mountain that you can't climb,

Making love helpless.

Time is the great river flowing east,

Taking love away.

Get away from me,

The farther, the better.

Then I can give up,

No longer clinging to you.

Facing the world alone,

I won't be sad any more.

Get away from me,

The farther, the better.

The memories will accompany me.

你对我的好
我永远记得
余生里慰藉寂寞

2018.6.23

I'll remember forever

Your past love to me

Which will comfort my loneliness for the rest of my life.

June 23 , 2018

今夜爱情已被遗忘

如果，夜是白天的延伸
她愿在夜色妖娆里
做一个风情女人
似真似假
似善似恶
是花也是毒蛇
是幸福也是痛苦
世上一定有个人
懂得她背后的泪痕
迷幻的灯光里
伴着暧昧的音乐
她袒露赤裸的灵魂
如果你是酒精
可以让她失去知觉
她愿来到你身旁
对着你调情歌唱
荷尔蒙的刺激
让人暂时告别忧伤
木讷可以变得风流倜傥
中规中矩可以变得放浪
爱情长着翅膀
飞离了她的梦乡
今夜，爱情已被遗忘

2018.6.11

Love Is Forgotten Tonight

If night is an extension of day,

She would like to be a flirt,

Being true or false,

Being good or evil,

Being a flower or a viper

And being happy or in pain.

There must be a man in the world

Who can understand her hidden tears.

In the psychedelic light,

With ambiguous music,

She bares her soul.

If you were alcohol,

You could make her lose consciousness.

She would like to come to you,

To flirt with you and sing to you.

The stimulation of hormones

Makes a person temporarily forget everything.

A dull man can become romantic and elegant.

A disciplined and intelligent person can become unrestrained.

Love has wings,

Flying away from her dreamland.

Tonight, love is forgotten.

June 11, 2018

潍坊的爱情

也不知怎么了
风筝广场的雕塑旁
你霸道地吻了我
我也轻轻回吻了你的脸
从此，思念的风筝
摇曳着飞上了天
俯瞰着潍坊的惊艳
突然天空涌上乌云一片
把广场上游玩的人群四下驱散
我多么希望
赶紧回到你身边
顺着思念的风筝线
我却看不到你焦急的脸
空旷的广场上只有雨花一片
原来你把风筝线拴在了灯杆
而你却早已躲远
空中的我不再挣扎回旋
暴风雨中慢慢落下
忘记曾经的蓝天
也许，只有暴风雨
才能洗刷掉蒙蔽爱情的尘烟
潍坊的春天，很短
潍坊的爱情，很闪

2018.6.1

Love in Weifang

I didn't know why
You kissed me peremptorily
Beside the statue in the kite square.
But I kissed your face gently in return.
From then on, my missing kite
Swayed gently in the sky,
Overlooking the amazing scenery of Weifang.
Suddenly the sky was covered with dark clouds,
Which dispersed the strolling people on the square.
How I wish you would have pulled me back
So I could return in your arms.
Following the string of the missing kite,
I couldn't see your anxious face
On the empty square only the rain flowers were blooming.
You tied the line to the light pole
And hid far away.
I didn't struggle or whirl around in the air any longer,
Slowly falling down in the storm
And forgetting the past blue sky
Perhaps, only the storm
Can wash away the dust that blinds love.
Spring in Weifang is short
And love in Weifang is quick.

June 1, 2018

最后的默契

相识那天，下着雨
你说，缘分靠运气
我说，你就是我的奇迹
二十年相依，彼此珍惜
你待我如初
我疼你入骨
以为，我俩能够走到底
可终究，你还是要离去
是时间冲淡了记忆
还是距离阻隔了希冀
没有争吵，没有哭泣
你不再找我，我也不再找你
你没拉黑我，我也没拉黑你
默默地，都在微信朋友圈里
也许，这是我俩最后的默契

2018.5.24

The Last Mutual Understanding

It was raining when we met.

You said destiny depended on luck

And I said you were my miracle.

We cherished each other for 20 years

During which you treated me as before.

I loved you from the bottom of my heart

And I thought we would be together to the end.

But in the end, you still had to leave me.

I don't know whether time diluted our love memory

Or the distance blocked the hope of our love.

Without arguing or crying,

You haven't contacted me and I haven't contacted you.

You haven't blocked me and I haven't blocked you on WeChat.

Both of us are on WeChat Moments silently.

Perhaps, this is our last mutual understanding.

May 24, 2018

离开我吧

亲爱的，告诉我吧
说你不再爱我
尽管选择最难听的话
我不会反驳
我都明白
我都会记得
请你不要沉默
你沉默的天空
会让我失去自我

亲爱的，离开我吧
离得越远越好
别回头别难过
你的心情我懂的
红尘世界里
我是凡人一个
无法给你想要的生活
就让距离和时间冲淡一切
只要你能忘记我

2017.5.22

Leave Me

My lover, please tell me,
Tell me you won't love me anymore.
You may choose the most hardhearted words,
But I will not refute you
Because I understand
And I'll remember them all.
Please don't be silent
Because the sky of your silence
Will make me lose myself.

My lover, please leave me,
The farther, the better.
Don't turn around or be sad.
I know your mood.
I'm an ordinary person
In the world.
I can not give you the life you want.
Let distance and time dilute everything
As long as you can forget me.

May 22, 2017

无言的结局

窗前，他满足的脸
外边的霓虹灯光
不时扫过他的裸体
忽明忽暗，就像
她喝醉酒的那晚
轻轻，她走上前
双手搂在他的腰间
熟悉的味道，再次弥漫
刚才的缠绵，暂时释放了
她多日的积怨
她求他，再住一晚
他回过头，敷衍
亲吻，她的脸
抱起她，又要走向床边
她奋力挣脱出来
他眼里飘忽的躲闪
让她心里再次生寒
爱情，不睁眼
相拥，也不暖
何谈一生的缘
她不是他
偶尔路过的客栈
她打开门，坐在床边
街上的霓虹灯依然璀璨

Wordless Ending

He was standing in front of the window
With satisfied look on his face.
The neon light spills onto his nude
Which made her
Think of the night she was drunk.
She quietly walked to him
And put her arms around his waist from behind.
Again the familiar smell diffused.
They made love just now and
Love made him forgive him.
So she begged him to stay for another night.
He turned back and apathetically kissed her face.
Then he picked her up,
Walking to the bed.
She struggled to free herself
Because from the dodge in his eyes,
She felt bitterly disappointed again.
He didn't love her,
So how could she get warm?
She wanted a lifetime love.
She didn't want to be the inn
Which he occasionally passed by.
She opened the door and sat down on the bed.
The neon lights in the streets were still bright.

外边传来了歌声
无言的结局
坐高铁误不了点

2018.5.21

From outside came a song

Which was called silent ending.

It wasn't too late for him to catch the high-speed train.

May 21, 2018

挂在梦里

那年，拿起懵懂的笔
春天里，画出了你美丽的羞涩
无能为力的年纪里
不经意，爱上了你
心中住满了，你的印记
却始终走不进，你的心底
你和他，若即若离
我却没有勇气，走上前去
自卑的我，不知如何和你说起
知道自己，没能力去爱你
不敢做恋人，只好哥们义气
不甘做朋友，深夜里总是恨自己
努力工作，充实自己
现在终于成了，你想要的样子
你却不是，原来的你
我俩之间，相隔了整个青春的距离
泪水，化作真诚的微笑
灿烂今生，爱的唯一
吃不到的葡萄，就挂在梦里
互不打扰，做最好的自己
时间和距离，会渐渐抚平记忆

2018.5.2

Hanging in Dream

I picked up the ignorant brush that year,

Painting your beautiful shyness in spring.

I loved you carelessly

At the age of incapacity.

You have been living in my heart

But I couldn't walk into yours.

You kept him at arm's length,

But I had no courage to step forward.

I was very self-abased and didn't know what to say to you

Because I didn't have the capacity to love you.

I dared not to be your lover, so I kept the brotherhood with you.

I was unwilling to be your friend, and I always hated myself at night.

I had to work hard to improve myself.

Now I've become the one you wanted,

But you are not the original you

Because there is a distance of youth time between us.

My tears turn into a genuine smile,

Brightening the only love in my life.

Hanging the grapes you can't eat in your dream,

We don't disturb each other and try to be the best we can be.

Time and distance will gradually smooth the memory.

May 2, 2018

求 你

求你，就今晚
让我小鸟依人
让我春藤缠树
那是我一生的期盼
临走，在我的伤口上
请你再撒把盐
给我最后的痛苦
好让我忘记从前
我会悄悄躲进孤独的房间
关上门窗，拉上窗帘
钻进被窝，蜷缩成一团
再不敢去面对，爱情的斑斓

2018.4.25

Begging You

I beg you, only tonight,
To let me be a little bird resting upon you
And twine you as a vine.
Because that is the expectation of my life.
Before your leave, please
Sprinkle salt on my cut again
To give me the ultimate pain
So that I can forget the past.
Then I will quietly hide in the lonely room,
Close the door and windows, pull the curtains closed,
Get under the sheets and curl up into a ball.
I dare not face the beauty of love again.

April 25, 2018

我爱过

知道，你不爱我
只求你，别对我说
卑微的我，躲在寂寞的角落
等你偶尔回头，用眼的余光扫过
那样我会激动万分，泪水瓢泼
告诉世界，我爱过

2017.10.9

I Have Loved

I know you do not love me
But I beg you not to tell me the truth.
My sense of inferiority makes me hide in the lonely corner,
Waiting for you to turn around occasionally and glance at me,
Then I will be so excited that tears will pour down,
And tell the world I have loved.

October 9, 2017

月　光

月光下，你曾信誓旦旦
亲吻着我说，爱我永远
我以为，我俩一定会
花好月圆，那是我一生的期盼
今晚，月儿圆了，你却走远
清冷的月光，洒在床边
我轻轻捧起，梦里你美丽的笑脸
灵性的月光啊
如果你是跳动的音符
怎能忘记，月光下的键盘
圣洁的月光啊
如果你是上苍派来的天仙
为何默默看着我，无言
多情的月光啊
如果你是天上倾泻下来的相思泪水
为何洗不尽，我的忧伤和思念
朦胧的月光啊
你迷惑了我的双眼
明天太阳一出
我知道你会变得陌生而遥远
但我还是记住了你的圆满
我宁愿一生相信你的谎言

2017.10.4

Moonlight

In the moonlight you kissed me,
Vowing to love me forever.
I thought you would marry me
But tonight the moon is round
And you have gone far away.
The cool moonlight is shining on the bedside
And I hold your beautiful smiling face in my dream.
My spiritual moonlight,
If you are the beating note,
How can you forget the keyboard in the moonlight?
My holy moonlight,
If you are an angel sent by God,
Why are you looking at me silently without any word?
My affectionate moonlight,
If you are the missing tears of love pouring down from the sky,
Why can't you wash away my sadness and missing away?
My hazy moonlight,
You have puzzled my eyes
And I know you will become
Strange and distant tomorrow
But I still think you are perfect.
I would rather believe your lies all my life.

October 4, 2017

失　恋

你把我的心
用力掏出
吸干了我
青春的血液
然后把干瘪的心
狠狠摔在
坚硬的石头上
用绝情踏碎
我卑微地弯腰
一块块捡起
小心翼翼拼凑起来
重新放进
没有了灵魂的躯体

2016.8.9

Lovelorn

You savagely pulled

My heart out

And sucked out

The blood of my youth.

Then you threw my shrivelled heart.

A hard stone

Was used to ruthlessly trample it,

Breaking it into pieces.

I stooped lowly

To pick up the debris,

Carefully putting the pieces together

And putting it into my body again

Which doesn't have a soul.

August 9, 2016

我曾遇见你

总想告诉你，我爱你
可我，终究还是没有勇气
你静静躺在联系人的名单里
彼此不再言语
忍不住写给你的微信
一次次被犹豫删除在深夜里
既然，不能在一起
那就留点念头，在梦里
因为，我曾遇见你

2017.9.20

I Have Met You

I always want to tell you I love you

But after all I still have no courage.

Your name is lying quietly in my list of the contacts

And we don't contact each other any longer.

The WeChat messages which I couldn't help writing occasionally to you

Were deleted again and again by my hesitation late at night.

Since we cannot love each other,

Let me keep you in my dream

Because I have met you.

September 20, 2017

承 受

你是手中一碗沸腾的开水
再烫，我也不敢放下
怕放下，人生酷热的沙漠里
再没有人能为我的爱情解渴

你是捧在手里的一只刺猬
扎透了我的心，还是不敢放下
怕放下，你会钻进污浊的草垛
我再也找不着

一次次吵架，一次次难过
一次次惦记着，一次次诉说
不要制造爱情的蹉跎
和风细雨才能滋润爱情的花朵

拉起警戒线，你却一次次越过
我只有步步后退
怕我的阻拦绊倒你
磕破你脸上浪漫的执着

即使你罪不可赦
我还是选择一次次把你放过
因为爱你，不想让你一个人
在红尘世界里随风漂泊

2017.8.4

Bearing

You are a bowl of boiling water in my hands.
No matter how hot it is, I don't put it down
Because if I put you down, I'm afraid that in the desert life
I'll never find the person like you to quench my thirst for love.

You are a hedgehog in my hands.
Though you have pierced my heart, I still can't put you down
Because I'm afraid if I put you down, you will get into the dirty haystack
And I can not find you anymore.

Quarrelling with you again and again , being sad over and over,
Caring about each other again and again and recounting our love,
Don't let love slip away
Because only a soft breeze and gentle drizzle can moisten the flowers of love.

I drew a line but you crossed it again and again
And I have to step back
Because I'm afraid that my obstruction will make you stumble,
Knocking the romantic obsession on your face.

Even if your crime is unforgivable,
I still choose to let you off again and again
Because I love you and I don't want you
To drift with the wind in the vanity fair alone.

August 4, 2017

当你不再爱我

当你不再爱我
我不会给你打电话
怕你不接时冰冷的沉默

当你不再爱我
我不会给你发信息
怕你偶尔的温存会让我更加寂寞

当你不再爱我
我不会问你为什么
怕我的呼吸也是多余的错

当你不再爱我
我不会再原谅你
怕二次伤害让我一错再错

当你不再爱我
我会选择平静的沉默
让伤口自己慢慢愈合

当你不再爱我
我会努力工作和生活
忙碌是转移痛苦最好的法则

When You Do Not Love Me Any Longer

When you do not love me any longer,
I will not call you
Because I'm afraid of your cold silence.

When you do not love me any longer,
I will not send you any messages
Because I'm afraid your occasional tenderness will make me even lonelier.

When you do not love me any longer,
I will not ask you why
Because I'm afraid my breathing is also an unnecessary mistake.

When you do not love me any longer,
I will not forgive you again
Because I'm afraid a second injury will make me repeat the mistake again.

When you do not love me any longer,
I will keep silent
And let the wound heal itself slowly.

When you do not love me any longer,
I will work hard and live
Because being busy is the best way to avoid pain.

当你不再爱我

我会默默祝福你

感谢你曾经带给我的快乐

2017.6.28

When you do not love me any longer,

I will bless you in silence,

And thank you for the happiness you once brought to me.

June 28, 2017

离　开

你离开得那么轻
一缕晚风
却把我从梦里吹醒

你离开得那么急
我跑出门外
已来不及哭泣

你离开的时间真巧
思念才进入梦里
刚要把你找到

你离开得那么干净
搜遍记忆
却找不到你的一点痕迹

2017.6.22

Leaving

You left so lightly.
But a night breeze
Woke me up from my dream.

You left so hurriedly.
I ran out the door
But I was too late to cry.

You left at an opportune time
Because my longing thoughts just ran into my dream
And I was just about to find you.

You left so neatly.
I searched my memory completely
But I could not find any trace of yours.

June 22, 2017

吞　噬

你的眼睛像海，深不见底
淹没了我，青春的孤寂
期盼着你，把我从大海里救起
你却驾驶着红色的快艇
来到我身旁，又残忍地离去
快艇激起的浪花，是我无言的泪滴
我不再挣扎，也不再呼吸
任凭无边的大海，慢慢吞噬自己
沉入海底，化作岩石
把我的爱恋，深深锁起
只有偶尔游过的小鱼
陪伴自己

2017.5.30

Swallowing

Your eyes are like the bottomless sea,

Drowning my lonely youth.

I am looking forward to you saving me from the sea.

You drove the red speedboat to me,

Passed by my side and left cruelly.

The waves you left are my silent tears.

I am no longer struggling or breathing,

Waiting for the boundless sea to swallow me slowly.

Sinking into the sea, I become a rock,

Locking up my deep love inside.

Only the small swimming fish passing by

Accompany me occasionally.

May 30, 2017

熬

以为，熬过去就好了
却没熬过时间和距离
你别哭，我抱不到你
就让我俩一别两宽，各生欢喜
放过你，我却放不过自己
孤独长夜醉倒在往事里
明天是否有人照顾你

2017.5.27

Staying and Persisting

I thought we would stick to our love

But we failed in the time and distance.

Please do not cry, because I can not hug you.

So let's break up and live respectively and happily.

I can let you go but I can't let myself go.

In the lonely night I'm drunk from past events,

Wondering whether someone will take care of you tomorrow.

May 27, 2017

拖　累

又来到熟悉的城市
我却不想告诉你
十五的月亮
淹没在都市璀璨的灯火里
曾经，单腿下跪的你
月亮下发誓非我不娶
幸福的泪水滋润着我干涸的过去
收拾起行李
我悄悄离去
不够勇敢的我
不想拖累年轻的你
如果有来生
我是否还会那样委屈自己
放弃有时是不得已
因为我依然那么爱你

2017.5.22

Encumbering

I came to the familiar city

But I didn't want to tell you.

The full moon

Is submerged in the bright light of the city.

Once, kneeling down on one knee before me,

You vowed to marry me in the moonlight

And I was moved to tears.

Picking up my luggage,

I left you quietly.

I did not want to encumber you

Because you were too young and I was not brave enough.

If there was a next life,

Will I receive your love?

Giving up is something you have to do sometimes

Because I still love you so much.

May 22, 2017

补　偿

知道，爱上你不会有结果
但思念的藤儿却一直不停生长
爬满了你家围墙
爬到了你家窗户上
看着你和别的女人上床
我不敢告诉你我的悲伤
我没有资格吃醋
更无法把你的余生拴在我身上
我爱的翅膀
已被自卑的泪水烫伤
无法与你一起飞向婚姻的殿堂
就让我在黑暗中等待
等到你老得起不了床
别的女人都离你而去
我会去把错过的爱情补偿
把你挥霍的灵魂送进天堂

2017.5.8

Compensation

I know falling in love with you will not bear fruit.

But my longing vine has been growing,

Covering your fence and

Climbing up to the window of your house.

Seeing you go to bed with other women,

I dare not tell you my sadness.

I'm not qualified to be jealous

And I can't tie you to me for the rest of your life.

I can not fly to the marriage hall with you

Because the wings of my love

Have been scalded by self-contemptuous tears.

Let me wait for you in the darkness

Until you are too old to get up by yourself.

Other women will be away from you

And I will go to compensate for the love we missed

And take your prodigal soul to the heaven.

May 8, 2017

爱情已睡去

一个手机屏幕

隔着我和你

想给你发个问候

我却没有勇气

怕我的问候

搅乱了你生活的安逸

寂静的夜晚

再次翻开聊天记录

重温我俩温柔的过去

惊奇地开始

默默地离去

是生活逼迫了你

还是爱情欺骗了自己

就让我把问候发到你的梦里

丢进时间的长河里

生活还要继续

爱情已睡去

2017.5.7

Love Has Gone to Sleep

A phone screen
Separates both of us.
I want to send you a greeting
But I have no courage
Because I'm afraid my greeting
Will disturb your carefree life.
In the silent night,
I open up our chat records again,
And recall our gentle past
Which started amazingly
But ended silently.
Has life forced you
Or has love deceived me?
Let me send you my greeting in your dream
And throw it into the long river of time.
Life will continue
But our love has gone to sleep.

May 7, 2017

视而不见

曾经
为一朵云驻足
因一滴雨感动
为一朵花低眉
因一缕春风相拥
我俩是世界上最温柔的人

如今
云儿优哉天边
花儿依旧灿烂
雨儿滴答一片
风儿轻轻拂面
你我各自摇上车窗
视而不见
我俩是最熟悉的陌生人
夜深人静时
我却突然泪流满面

2017.5.5

Turning a Blind Eye

Previously
We stopped for a cloud
And we were moved by a drop of rain.
We lowered our heads for a flower
And embraced in the spring breeze.
We were the gentlest lovers in the world.

Now,
The clouds are leisurely floating in the sky
And the flowers are in full bloom.
The raindrops are falling on the ground
And the wind is gently touching my face.
We roll up our car windows respectively
And turn a blind eye to each other.
We are the most familiar strangers.
When all is still at night,
I suddenly burst into tears.

May 5, 2017

车　票

弯腰，悄悄捡起
一枚枚失望的硬币
放进宽大的裤兜里
终于有一天攒够了
用来买了一张离开的车票
一个人站在车站
眼泪还是不争气
飘落在秋风里
模糊了善变的你
还有当初那个奋不顾身的自己

2017.5.3

Ticket

Stooping down, I quietly picked up
The disappointing coins one by one,
And put them into my large pocket.
Finally I saved enough money one day
And used the coins to buy a ticket to leave.
Standing at the station alone,
I couldn't help crying.
My tears were falling in the autumn wind,
Blurring the fickle you
And the original self who loved you furiously.

May 3, 2017

等

等，等你邂逅我

等，等你天天约我

等，等你主动说爱我

等，等你把我俩的岁月蹉跎

等，等我习惯了绝望和寂寞

等，等你我相互忘记爱的承诺

2017.5.2

Waiting

Waiting, I'm waiting for you to meet me by chance.

Waiting, I'm waiting for you to go on a date with me.

Waiting, I'm waiting for you to take the initiative to tell me you love me.

Waiting, I'm waiting for you to waste our time together.

Waiting, I'm waiting for me to get used to despair and loneliness.

Waiting, I'm waiting for us to forget our promise of our love to each other.

May 2, 2017

中年爱情

曾经，我把一切放入心中
梦、春雨和星星
落叶、老歌和合影
它们是我俩爱的见证

现在，我把它们从心中掏空
我把梦系在浪花上
让海鸥追逐爱的懵懂
我把春雨洒在田野
看你花枝招展笑盈盈
我把星星泡在一杯茶里
品味青春爱情的交融
我把落叶夹在日记中
风干了往日甜蜜的憧憬
我把那首老歌系在你的窗棂
深夜醒来抚慰爱的伤痛
我把咱俩的合影挂在白云上
渐渐飘远，无影无踪

此刻，我的心里万籁俱静
茫茫宇宙里，唯有上帝召唤的声音
闭上双眼，让爱的灵魂向着天堂飞行
那里永远春暖花开，没有爱的寒冷

2017.4.6

Love of Middle Age

Once, I put everything into my heart,
Such as a dream, spring rain, stars,
A fallen leaf, an old song and photos,
Because they are witnesses of our love.

Now, I empty them out of my heart.
I tie the dream to the waves,
Letting the seagulls ignorantly chase love.
I spread the spring rain in the field,
Appreciating your gorgeous beauty and smiling.
I put the stars in a cup of tea,
Tasting the blend of young love.
I put the leaf in a diary
Which is dried up by the sweet longing of the past.
I tie the old song to your window lattice
Which soothes the pain of love when you wake up late at night.
I hang our group photos on the clouds
Which gradually drift away without a trace.

At the moment, my heart is so quiet.
There is only the voice of God calling in the vast universe.
Closing my eyes, my soul of love is flying toward the heaven.
It is always spring and there is no cold there.

April 6, 2017

不见了

不知什么时候，你就不见了
以为你变成了，湖边柳树梢上的春风
你却拂过水面，消失得无影无踪

不知什么时候，你就不见了
以为你变成了，河边盛开的花丛
你却很快凋零，花瓣随着溪水远行

不知什么时候，你就不见了
以为你变成了，床边寂寞的梦
你却让我早上头痛，模糊了你的笑容

2017.4.5

Gone

I do not know when you left.

I thought you became the spring breeze around the willow trees by the lake

But the spring breeze kissed the water and then disappeared without a trace.

I do not know when you left.

I thought you became a flower on the riverbank

But the flowers withered quickly and fell into the stream.

I do not know when you left.

I thought you became a lonely dream

But you gave me a headache in the morning, blurring your smiling face.

April 5, 2017

风干的玫瑰花瓣

春天的早上，我打开窗子
斑斓的阳光，洒满书房
舒缓的音乐，随着鸟语流淌
取下书架上那一摞珍藏，坐在藤椅上
茶几上的香茗，我却忘了品尝
拿起那本厚厚的日记，纸张已发黄
不经意翻开厚重的记忆
一片夹在书层里的玫瑰花瓣
悄悄滑落到地板上
我小心捡起，仔细观赏
它褪去了鲜艳的色彩，却依然馨香
轻轻抿一口香茗
却分明闻到你汗味的芬芳
看着日记，泪落两行
模糊了你性感的脸庞
以为我俩，会地久天长
可时间和距离却将我阻挡
也许我不够坚强
没有手拉手的空间
宁愿你我相距万里长
远方的你，是否能理解我
难言的悲伤

2017.4.3

A Dried Rose Petal

In the spring morning, I opened the window

And the gorgeous sunshine filled my study,

With soothing music and the singing of birds.

After taking the books off the shelves, I was seated in the rattan chair,

Forgetting to sip the tea on the tea table.

I picked up a thick diary which had become yellow.

I opened the heavy memory inadvertently,

And rose petal in the book

Fell quietly to the floor.

I picked up the petal and looked at it carefully

It was still fragrant but its bright color had faded.

Taking a sip of tea,

Clearly I smelled the fragrance of your sweat.

Reading the diary, my eyes were full of tears

Which blurred your sexy face.

I thought we would love each other forever

But time and distance stopped me.

Maybe because I wasn't strong enough.

There was no room for us to love,

I'd rather be far away from you.

Can you understand

My unspeakable sadness from far away?

April 3, 2017

罂粟花

心底山谷间
一株罂粟花，静静生长
亭亭玉立的身姿
闺中少女般羞涩缠绵
纯色的花瓣，艳丽的容颜
勾住了我孤独灵魂的双眼
轻轻靠近，慢慢吸吮
迷幻了寂寞的夜晚
沉醉迷恋中
忘记世间哀怨
知道，她花枝招展下面
藏着诀别的梦魇
知道，离开她的瞬间
必定是蚀骨入髓的痛感
知道，爱上她
是塔纳托斯的呼唤
心甘情愿，闭上双眼
坠入死亡之恋
用青春的鲜血
浇灌她妖艳的花朵
绽放在我荒芜的坟边
我的灵魂不再孤单

2017.3.30

Poppy Flower

In the valley of my heart,

A poppy flower is quietly growing.

Having a graceful posture,

She is as shy as a girl.

Her pure color petals and bright face

Caught the eyes of my lonely soul.

Approaching her gently and kissing her slowly,

In the psychedelic and lonely night,

I'm indulged in the obsession

Of forgetting the sorrow of the world.

I know her farewell nightmare

Is hidden under her beautiful dress.

I know when she leaves me,

The acute pain will go into my bone marrow.

I know falling in love with her

Is the call of Tarnatos.

I'm willing to close my eyes,

Falling into the death of love.

I use the blood of my youth

To water her beautiful flower

Which will bloom near my desolate grave

And my soul will never be lonely.

March 30, 2017

炸酱面

周末回家，妈妈做好了
我最爱吃的炸酱面
捧着饭碗，想起我俩
第一次在面馆吃饭
那天，你特别好看
我吃得特别慢
别发呆，赶快趁热吃完
妈妈又开始唠叨没完
这次，我没有心烦
些许感动，心底发酸
真想抱住妈妈
像小时候那样
在妈妈怀里哭个没完
吃了几口，跑回房间
翻开你的微信留言
从头看一遍，傻笑
枕头上你留下的味道
淡淡，感觉比蜜甜
远方的你，请告诉我
来生，我俩是否还有缘

2016.6.17

Bean Sauce Noodles

I went home at the weekend and my mum
Cooked my favorite bean sauce noodles.
Holding the bowl, I thought of
Our first date in a noodle shop.
That day you were particularly handsome
And I ate the noodles especially slowly.
Do not daydream and eat it while it's hot.
Mum began to nag endlessly again.
This time I was not upset
But felt a little moved and heartsick.
I want to hold my mum
Like I did when I was a child
And cry endlessly in my mum's arms.
Having eaten a few bites, I ran back to the room,
I read your previous WeChat message
From start to finish, giggling.
Smelling the fragrance which you left on the pillow,
I felt sweeter than honey.
Please tell me from far away,
In the next life, whether we will still be together.

June 17, 2016

不再把你寻找

趁着春光正好
趁着风儿不燥
趁着记忆不老
来到你的城市
走你熟悉的街道
吃你最爱的水饺
学着你的样子
在初识的那个咖啡馆
来个微笑的自拍照
寄给梦里的你
告诉你
我将不再把你寻找

2017.3.15

I will Not Look For You Again

Taking the advantage of the light,

While the wind is not dry,

While the memories haven't faded,

I came to your city.

Walking in your familiar street,

Eating your favorite dumplings,

I did what you had done.

At the café where we first met,

I took a photo of myself, smiling.

I'll send the photo to you in my dream

And tell you

I will not look for you again.

March 15, 2017

别 离

抬起眼睛，不敢看你
身边匆匆走过的游客
带走了你不着边际的话语
南卡罗来纳州的飓风
吹着你美丽的面容
机场广播里传来
飞机快要起飞的消息
你的眼圈开始发红
冬天里不该有雨滴
甩开，你要拉我的手
开车狂奔向市里
请原谅我的无礼
车里，泪水已打湿了
你为我买的衬衣
昨天接到你的电话
其实，我还在外地
只为了能看你一眼
匆匆赶回我俩熟悉的小区
已离异的你，不会知道
我还是单身一人
如果，真的后会有期
难道又是七年的分离

2017.2.28

Parting

Looking up, I dare not look at you.

Tourists passing by

Took away your meaningless words.

Hurricane in South Carolina

Was blowing your beautiful face.

An announcement was broadcast in the airport.

The plane was about to take off.

You wanted to cry,

But there should not be raindrops in winter.

You grabbed my hand but I pushed your hand out of the way

And drove madly to the city.

Please forgive me for being rude.

The shirt you bought for me

Was wet with my tears.

When I received your phone call yesterday,

In fact, I was still in another place.

In order to see you,

I hurried back to our familiar neighborhood.

You are divorced but you don't know

I am still single.

If we meet again some day,

Will we be separated for another seven years?

February 28, 2017

别来打扰我

奢望过，痴迷过
深爱过，快乐过
一切都是错
彷徨过，挣扎过
伤害过，抑郁过
彼此失去了联络
铃声响起，陌生的号码
拿起手机，熟悉的声音
惊讶，沉默
放手了，为何还不舍
眼泪，悄悄溢满眼窝
拒绝，拉黑
宁愿孤傲地单身
也不愿委屈拍拖
宁愿做大龄剩女
也不想做短婚弃妇
缘分，已从指间滑落
除了记忆，还能剩下什么
不想知道，谁对谁错
分手了，别来打扰我
习惯了一个人生活
习惯了花开花落

2018.7.2

Don't Bother Me

I had extravagant hopes and infatuation.

I loved deeply and I was happy.

But now everything is wrong.

I hesitated and struggled.

I was hurt and depressed.

We lost touch with each other.

The phone rang and it was a strange number.

I answered the phone, hearing a familiar voice.

I was surprised and kept silence.

We broke up, so why did you call me?

My eyes were full of tears.

I rejected the call and blocked the number.

I would rather be aloof and proud

Than date with you.

I would rather be a single woman

Than become a deserted wife wth a short marriage.

The happy fate has slipped through our fingers.

There is nothing left but memories.

I don't want to know who is right or who is wrong.

We broke up and so do not bother me.

I am used to living alone

With the time going on.

July 2, 2018

第四辑　执子之手

最后的浪漫

找一汪汩汩的清泉
洗去脸上的疲倦
让青春美丽重现
寻一片最美的红叶
贴在你褪色的嘴唇
把生命的火焰重新点燃
剪下两片垂柳的叶子
粘在你起皱的眉骨处
妩媚心中的春天
采撷两滴滚动的晨露
滴进你浑浊的双眼
纯净你的晚年
祈求上天派来两只玉兔
卧在你干瘪下垂的胸前
让生命再次变得丰满性感
寻一个黑色的瀑布
替换你稀疏的白发
飘逸出生命的灿烂
觅一处世外桃源
与你漫步生命的秋天
体验人生最后的浪漫

2017.9.19

The Last Romance

I want to look for a clear gurgling spring

To wash away the exhaustion on your face,

Which can make you young and beautiful again.

I want to look for the most beautiful red leaf

And stick it on your faded lips

To reignite the passion in your life.

I want to get two weeping willow leaves

And paste them to your wrinkled eyebrows

to charm the spring in your heart.

I want to collect two drops of rolling dew

And put them into your cloudy eyes

To purify your old age.

I pray that God would send two jade rabbits

To lie down on your withered and drooping chest

To make your life full and sexy once again.

I want to look for a black waterfall

To replace your thin gray hair,

Which can make your life elegant.

I want to look for the land of idyllic beauty

To wander with you in the autumn life

And experience the last romance of life.

September 19, 2017

你让我的心变小了

亲爱的，你的存在
是我今生永恒的梦
流连忘返，乐在其中
曾以为世界很美
曾以为自己志向远大
但，自从遇到你
才知道，你的世界
才是世上最美的风景
才知道，拥有你
才是我最大的志向
才知道，我的心那么小
小得只能容下你
容不下对别的女人丁点的觊觎
我哪里也不想去
因为最美的时光
就是一生守着你
说许多话，做许多事
每天腻歪在一起
直到我俩都走不动了
我就用老人车带着你
一起向天堂驶去

2018.5.23

You Make My Heart Become Small

Darling, your existence

Is the eternal dream of my life.

It is enjoyable and makes me forget to return.

I thought the world was beautiful

And I was very ambitious.

Only when I met you

Did I know that your world

Is the most beautiful scenery in the world.

Only then did I know my greatest ambition

Is to have you.

Only then did I know my heart is so small.

There is only room for you

And there is no room to covet other women.

I don't want to go anywhere

Because the most beautiful time

Is to stay with you all my life,

Talking a lot and doing many things.

We'll be together every day

Until neither of us can walk,

Then I'll take you with me to heaven

In the old man's car.

May 23, 2018

还　账

爱情账户上
我欠你太多
没能力还你
就把我生命的余额
我的后半生给你

2016.8.7

Repaying

I owe you too much

In the love account.

I have no ability to repay you,

So I have to give you my life as balance,

That is to say, I owe you the rest of life.

August 7, 2016

再 见

如果，我的生命
即将停止生长
请不要悲伤
我不要 ICU
也不想喝药汤
只希望你在身旁
给我穿上漂亮的衣裳
鲜花在屋内飘香
音乐在耳旁悠扬
阳光透过花窗照在身上
躺在你怀里
一起回忆美好的过往
微笑着和你说再见
慢慢闭上眼睛
满足而安详
走在你前头
只为在天堂里铺好你我永远的婚床
等明日我俩一起进入梦乡
爱情的本质是快乐
爱情的永恒在天堂

2017.10.7

Goodbye

If my life

Is about to stop growing,

Please do not be sad.

I need neither ICU

Nor medicine.

I only wish that you would stay with me

And dress me in beautiful clothes.

The house is full of the fragrance of flowers

While melodious music is in my ears.

The sun is shining through the window, illuminating my body.

I lie in your arms,

Recalling our sweet past with you.

I smilingly say goodbye to you.

Being satisfied and serene,

I slowly closed my eyes.

I go to heaven earlier than you because

I'd like to make our eternal bed well in advance,

Waiting for us to go to dreamland tomorrow.

The essence of love is happiness

And love is eternal in heaven.

October 7, 2017

每天告诉你

遇上你，是我的福气
不是有缘，我俩不会在一起
每天告诉你，我想你

把羞涩和木讷从心里抹去
嘴上涂上世界上最甜的蜜
每天告诉你，我爱你

把梦里的爱情
浸泡在一日三餐锅碗瓢盆里
每天告诉你，我疼你

把自己最后的力气聚集
伺候老来蹒跚的你
每天告诉你，我扶你

2017.5.6

Telling You Every Day

Meeting you is a blessing.
It is the destiny that brings us together.
I will tell you every day that I miss you.

Erasing shyness and dullness from my heart
And using the most beautiful words,
Every day I will tell you that I love you.

Putting my dreamy love
In the daily necessities,
Every day I will tell you that I cherish you.

Gathering my last strength,
I will serve you when you become old and walk unsteadily
And to tell you every day that I will help you.

May 6, 2017

地老天荒

把迁就和疼爱的聘礼搬上婚车
去迎娶你，我可爱的新娘
你把温暖的心作为嫁妆
和我携手走入婚姻的殿堂
油盐酱醋茶的生活里
和你闲聊，陪你歌唱
一个温情的拥抱
赛过荣华富贵的天堂
偶尔的吵嘴生气
总是被你调皮地轻松释放
如今你我已白发苍苍
我依然爱你，如当初那样
既然选择了承诺
就要相守地久天长

2017.4.12

Everlasting

Getting into the wedding car with loving betrothal gifts,

I drive to marry you, my lovely bride.

Bringing me a warm heart as a dowry,

You go into the marriage hall with me hand in hand.

In our daily life,

I chat with you and sing to you.

A warm embrace

Is better than the rank and riches of paradise.

Occasional quarrels

Are always easily released by your naughty.

Now we are grey-haired

And I still love you as before.

Since I have made a promise,

I will stay with you all my life.

April 12, 2017

原谅我

远远地，你走来，不声不响
把一束鲜花，轻轻放在我身旁
你还是那么漂亮，温柔、性感的魅力无处掩藏
一袭黑色的衣服，衬托着你梨花带雨的模样
不要为我烧香，那会熏黑了你美丽的脸庞
也不要为我烧纸钱，天堂里我的钱一箱一箱
亲爱的人啊，不要难过，也不要悲伤
你看你送给我的鲜花，艳丽芬芳
多么想，再次亲吻你俊俏的脸庞
给你我全部的爱，那本是上帝对我最大的奖赏
原谅我，不该留下你一个人，在这冷漠的世界上
让你过早学会，一个人刚强
如果有一双肩膀替我，为你把风雨阻挡
我愿看到你在他的怀里，小鸟依人的模样
如果那样，我就变成天上那颗最亮的星星
悄悄挂在，你再婚的窗户上
太阳一出，我就躲藏在天幕后方
不想让你看到，我的悲伤
天堂里，春暖花开
没有疾病，也没有世俗偏见的阻挡
我等着你，等着与你续缘，地老天荒

2017.4.4

344

Forgive Me

Nearer and nearer, you come quietly

And softly put a bouquet of flowers in front of me.

You are still so beautiful and gentle. Your sexy charm has nowhere to hide.

Dressed in black, you are in tears.

Do not light incense for me because it will blacken your beautiful face.

Do not burn paper money for me because I have many boxes of money in heaven.

Darling, do not be sorry and do not be sad.

You see the flowers you gave me are so beautiful and fragrant.

How I want to kiss your beautiful face again

Because giving you all my love is God's greatest reward for me.

Forgive me for going to the heaven first.

I leave you alone in this indifferent world and cause you to learn be strong.

If there is a pair of shoulders to replace me, to block the wind and rain from you,

I would like to see you in his arms like a little bird resting upon him.

If so, I will become the brightest star in the sky,

Quietly hanging on the window.

When the sun rises, I will hide behind the sky,

Because I do not want you to see my sadness.

In heaven, spring flowers are blooming.

There is no diseases or worldly prejudice.

I'm waiting for you to continue our destiny, waiting for you to the end of time.

April 4, 2017

后　记

为了自己爱的人
为了爱自己的人
为了喜欢英语的人
为了自己梦里的心愿
采撷四年中点滴感动
写下一地葱茏的稚嫩爱情诗
期盼你我的爱情永恒
感谢朱建霞和傅彩霞的无私帮助
感谢美国专家 Kellie 细心的英文修改
感谢爱人和儿子的理解和支持

2019.4.9

图书在版编目（ＣＩＰ）数据

香爱：汉英对照 / 曾抗著. -- 武汉：长江文艺出版社，2020.12

ISBN 978-7-5702-1439-6

Ⅰ. ①香… Ⅱ. ①曾… Ⅲ. ①诗集－中国－当代－汉、英 Ⅳ. ①I227

中国版本图书馆 CIP 数据核字（2020）第 004636 号

责任编辑：胡　璇　　　　　　　责任校对：毛　娟
封面设计：吕袭明　　　　　　　责任印制：邱　莉　　王光兴

出版：　长江出版传媒　　长江文艺出版社

地址：武汉市雄楚大街 268 号　　　邮编：430070

发行：长江文艺出版社

http://www.cjlap.com

印刷：武汉市首壹印务有限公司

开本：640 毫米×970 毫米　　　1/16　　印张：22.625　　插页：2 页
版次：2020 年 12 月第 1 版　　　2020 年 12 月第 1 次印刷
行数：8748 行

定价：39.00 元